I0749318

Two Cats & Other Stories

Publications from
The Scheherazade Foundation

The Secrets of Scheherazade
An Ordered Experience
Tale of a Lantern & Other Stories
The Elephant & The Tortoise & Other Stories
The Monkey's Fiddle & Other Stories
Ghost of the Violet Well & Other Stories
Many Wise Fools & Other Stories
The Frog Prince & Other Stories
The Three Lemons & Other Stories
The Twelve-Headed Griffin & Other Stories
The Antelope Boy & Other Stories
Why the Fish Laughed & Other Stories
Two Cats & Other Stories
Three Stories
The Twilight of the Gods & Other Stories
The Son of Seven Queens & Other Stories
The Moon Maiden & Other Stories
The Metamorphosis & Other Stories
The Celestial Sisters & Other Stories
Tales From the Arabian Nights I
East of the Sun, West of the Moon & Other Stories
The Well at the End of the World & Other Stories

Two Cats & Other Stories

Edited & Introduced by

TAHIR SHAH

The Scheherazade Foundation

The Scheherazade Foundation CIC
85 Great Portland Street
London
W1W 7LT
United kingdom
www.SF.Charity
info@SF.Charity

First published by The Scheherazade Foundation CIC, 2023

TWO CATS
&
OTHER STORIES

Two Cats
Folk-lore & Legends: Oriental
Charles John Tibbitts
J. B. Lippincott
1892

Punchkin
Old Deccan Days
Mary Frere
John Murray Ltd.
1929

Judgements of Karakash
Folklore of the Holy Land
J. E. Hanauer
Duckworth & Co.
1907

The Story of Pretty Goldilocks
The Blue Fairy Book
Andrew Lang
Longmans, Green & Co.
1889

The Hero Twins
Pueblo Indian Folk-Stories
Charles Lummis
The Century Company Inc.
1910

The Disobedient Daughter Who Married a Skull
Folk Stories from Southern Nigeria
Elphinstone Dayrell
Longmans, Green and Co.
1910

The Enchanted Wine-jug
Korean Tales
Horace Newton Allen
G. P. Putnam's Sons
1889

The Legend of the Wooden Shoe
Dutch Fairy Tales for Young Folks
William Elliot Griffis
Thomas Y. Crowell & Co.
1918

Rabbit & the Moon-man
Canadian Fairy Tales
Cyrus Macmillan
The Bodley Head Ltd.
1922

The Story of Ivan & the Daughter of the Sun
Cossack Fairy Tales & Folk Tales
R. Nisbet Bain
George G. Harrap & Co.
1916

The Ivory City & Its Fairy Princess
Indian Fairy Tales
Joseph Jacobs
G. P. Putnam's Sons
1910

The Death 'Bree'
Folk-lore & Legends: Scotland
Charles John Tibbitts
W. W. Gibbings, London
1889

A CIP catalogue record for this title is available from the British Library.

ISBN 978-1-915311-40-5

Contents

Series Introduction

FROM EARLIEST CHILDHOOD, I was told stories.

Of course I was – most children are told stories.

After all, telling children stories is one of the foundations that makes their early experiences a childhood.

But as I think back to the first years of my own life, I find myself reeling from the sheer quantity of stories my infant ears took in.

Whereas other children my age were told stories for amusement, my parents (and the people they associated with) recounted the endless streams of tales for a different reason.

In their opinion, stories – and the ability to tell them – were part of an ancient alchemy… a way of processing complex ideas, of solving problems, and of developing the human mind.

My father, the writer and thinker Idries Shah, believed that folklore was the single most important breakthrough ever developed by the human species. The way he saw it, the rise of stories was as consequential as the development of the languages in which they were told.

He would say that, without stories and storytelling, humanity would never have evolved in the way that it has – and that the folktales, which form a bedrock of ancient societies, are more precious than any physical artefact unearthed on an archaeological dig.

As the years of my own childhood slipped by, I found myself unbothered to work out the hidden layers within treasuries of stories – what my father called 'instruction manuals to the world'. Like everyone else, I simply absorbed the individual tales, delighting in them.

And that's it – the key point, the genius of stories and storytelling.

It's a thing I only grasped in adulthood… something that fascinates me deeply.

In the same way you can jump into a car and drive across the country without giving a second thought to the engine or how it works, you can appreciate stories without understanding the hidden layers and devices that make them what they are.

Stories are all around us.

They're in the TV and movies we so adore, in the video games we play, and of course in the books we read. They're in newspapers and magazines, too; in the conversations we share with old friends, and with new ones. They're on our mobile phones, in aeroplanes, in submarines, and even in our dreams.

Our obsession with, and craving for, stories rests squarely with the way we are so absorbed by them, just as it does with the way we don't need to continually consider how and why they work.

Throughout my life, I've devoted an increasing amount of time to gathering stories from all corners of the world.

It began in my late teens, when I began to criss-cross the continents in a crazed preoccupation with folklore. I developed a first-hand love affair with societies that, over millennia, gave birth to their own astonishing traditions of stories and storytelling.

Most of the time, when reading or listening to stories, we forget that these tales have been shaped through the passage of time. Like pebbles in a river smoothed by rushing waters, they were honed through centuries of telling and retelling.

When I was twelve years old, my father published a masterwork, *World Tales*. The first edition was very large and featured hundreds of original illustrations. The book was unlike any that had come before, for it detailed the provenance and history of each story told.

At bedtime one night, he presented me with an advanced copy. For as long as I could remember, my father had been talking about the project.

Having an actual copy in my hands at last was thrilling beyond words.

Peering down at me sternly, my father said:

'This is far more than a book, Tahir Jan. It's the foundation stone of a great building… a building that *is* human culture. As you grow older, and as you go out into the world, you will understand that the folklores contained between the covers of *World Tales* have brought amusement and educated, and have solved problems when they were needed most of all.'

My father was right.

When I eventually headed out into the wilds of the world for the first time, I discovered the stories contained in *World Tales* for myself, along with a great many more. Just as he said, the stories published in his treasury were the warp and weft threads of society. Stories are the matrix on which culture itself is based – a framework that enables daily life to continue as smoothly as it does.

In this series of books, we have drawn together stories from all over the world. It's a mission begun decades ago by *World Tales*.

Some of the pieces will be known to you, and others will not.

Some will be easy to comprehend, while others will be challenging, or even nonsensical.

I'd now like to note something else…

The Occidental world seems to assume stories must appear in certain regimented ways – presented with a well-defined beginning, a middle, and an end. You know what I mean: the protagonist winning against all odds, and the happy ending to it all.

In the ancient tradition of teaching stories, the kind recounted for an eternity around campfires in the desert and in longhouses deep in the jungle, there's no such standardisation.

Rather, there's usually a hotchpotch of conflicting threads: stories without a straight linear narrative but with an underlying turbulence that gets the reader, or the listener, to sit up and think.

At The Scheherazade Foundation, we are preoccupied with the way we can extract knowledge from stories – either deliberately, or in a less structured way.

We hold the firm opinion that, in order to remove the marrow from the bone stories are best served up in the way as they were passed from one generation to the next throughout human history.

In this series, we have drawn together tales that were gathered in particular during the nineteenth and early twentieth centuries. Spanning a vast range of cultures, they offer an extraordinary glimpse into the societies from which they are drawn – societies that were often changed shortly afterwards by social upheaval, technologies, and war.

Indeed, the fact any of them were recorded at all is a thing of wonder.

Intriguingly, some of the tales will now appear dated because vocabulary and writing styles have altered. But the fact that they seem old-fashioned is of great interest – proof of the way stories are constantly changing and evolving from one era to the next.

Over the last thirty years, I've gathered hundreds of tales on my own journeys, most of them spoken directly into my ears by storytellers and fellow travellers, by wizened old men in the middle of nowhere, and by anyone else good enough to indulge my pleas.

On all those zigzagging adventures, one story sticks out, tantalising me whenever I turn it around my head.

It was called 'The Man Who Turned into a Cat'.

The reason I mention it here is not because it was an especially fine tale, but rather because, from that moment, it affected the way I perceive the world.

It was as though I were a lock and that, by hearing the tale, a key had been slipped into me and turned.

Since first receiving it, I've never been quite the same, my state of consciousness having been flipped inside out.

The fellow traveller who recounted 'The Man Who Turned into a Cat' was lost in shadow, no more than a fragment of his left cheek protruding shyly into the light.

We were sitting on low divans in a teahouse in the ancient Afghan city of Herat.

When the tale had been whispered, I sat there in silence for a long while.

'What have you done to me?' I asked after a long pause.

The fellow traveller offered half a smile.

'*I* didn't do anything,' he replied. 'It's the story that's affected you – a story that I myself first heard when I was a child playing in the orchards of Balkh.'

Peering into the shadow, my eyes widened.

'I don't understand,' I said feebly. 'After all, it's not an especially grand story. There wasn't even a jinn.'

The traveller's mouth eased out from the shadows.

Very slowly, it grinned.

'Tales containing the greatest sustenance for a soul speak in the softest voice,' he said.

Tahir Shah

Two Cats

IN FORMER DAYS there was an old woman, who lived in a hut more confined than the minds of the ignorant, and more dark than the tombs of misers. Her companion was a cat, from the mirror of whose imagination the appearance of bread had never been reflected, nor had she from friends or strangers ever heard its name.

It was enough that she now and then scented a mouse, or observed the print of its feet on the floor; when, blessed by favouring stars or benignant fortune, one fell into her claws,

'She became like a beggar who discovers a treasure of gold; Her cheeks glowed with rapture, and past grief was consumed by present joy.'

This feast would last for a week or more; and while enjoying it she was wont to exclaim:

'Am I, O God, when I contemplate this, in a dream or awake? Am I to experience such prosperity after such adversity?'

But as the dwelling of the old woman was in general the mansion of famine to this cat, she was always complaining, and forming extravagant and fanciful schemes. One day, when reduced to extreme weakness, she, with much exertion, reached the top of the hut; when there she observed a cat stalking on the wall of a neighbour's house, which, like a fierce tiger, advanced with measured steps, and was so loaded with flesh that she could hardly raise her feet. The old woman's friend was amazed to see one of her own species so fat and sleek, and broke out into the following exclamation:

'Your stately strides have brought you here at last; pray tell me from whence you come? From whence have you arrived with so lovely an appearance? You look as if from the banquet of the Khan of Khatai. Where have you acquired such a comeliness? And how came you by that glorious strength?'

The other answered,

'I am the sultan's crumb-eater. Each morning, when they spread the convivial table, I attend at the palace, and there exhibit my address and courage. From among the rich meats and wheat-cakes I cull a few choice morsels; I then retire and pass my time till next day in delightful indolence.'

The old dame's cat requested to know what rich meat was, and what taste wheat-cakes had?

'As for me,' she added, in a melancholy tone, 'during my life I have neither eaten nor seen anything but the old woman's gruel and the flesh of mice.'

The other, smiling, said,

'This accounts for the difficulty I find in distinguishing you from a spider. Your shape and stature is such as must make the whole generation of cats blush; and we must ever feel ashamed while you carry so miserable an appearance abroad. You certainly have the ears and tail of a cat, but in other respects you are a complete spider.

'Were you to see the sultan's palace, and to smell his delicious viands, most undoubtedly those withered bones would be restored; you would receive new life; you would come from behind the curtain of invisibility into the plane of observation.

'When the perfume of his beloved passes over the tomb of a lover, is it wonderful that his putrid bones should be re-animated?'

The old woman's cat addressed the other in the most supplicating manner:

'O my sister!' she exclaimed, 'have I not the sacred claims of a neighbour upon you? Are we not linked in the ties of kindred? What prevents your giving a proof of friendship, by taking me with you when next you visit the palace? Perhaps from your favour plenty may flow to me, and from your patronage I may attain dignity and honour. Withdraw not from the friendship of the honourable; abandon not the support of the elect.'

The heart of the sultan's crumb-eater was melted by this pathetic address; she promised her new friend should accompany her on the next visit to the palace. The latter, overjoyed, went down immediately from the terrace, and communicated every particular to the old woman, who addressed her with the following counsel:

'Be not deceived, my dearest friend, with the worldly language you have listened to; abandon not your corner of content, for the cup of the covetous is only to be filled by the dust of the grave, and the eye of cupidity and hope can only be closed by the needle of mortality and the thread of fate.

It is content that makes men rich. Mark this, ye avaricious, who traverse the world: He neither knows nor pays adoration to his God who is dissatisfied with his condition and fortune.'

But the expected feast had taken such possession of poor puss's imagination, that the medicinal counsel of the old woman was thrown away.

'The good advice of all the world is like wind in a cage, or water in a sieve, when bestowed on the headstrong.'

To conclude: next day, accompanied by her companion, the half-starved cat hobbled to the sultan's palace. Before this unfortunate wretch came, as it is decreed that the covetous shall be disappointed, an extraordinary event had occurred, and, owing to her evil destiny, the water of disappointment was poured on the flame of her immature ambition.

The case was this: a whole legion of cats had the day before surrounded the feast, and made so much noise that they disturbed the guests; and in consequence the sultan had ordered that some archers armed with bows from Tartary should, on this day, be concealed, and that whatever cat advanced into the field of valour, covered with the shield of audacity, should, on eating the first morsel, be overtaken with their arrows.

The old dame's puss was not aware of this order. The moment the flavour of the viands reached her, she flew like an eagle to the place of her prey.

Scarcely had the weight of a mouthful been placed in the scale to balance her hunger, when a heart-dividing arrow pierced her breast.

A stream of blood rushed from the wound. She fled, in dread of death, after having exclaimed,

'Should I escape from this terrific archer, I will be satisfied with my mouse and the miserable hut of my old mistress. My soul rejects the honey if accompanied by the sting. Content, with the most frugal fare, is preferable.'

From: Folk-lore & Legends: Oriental

Punchkin

Once upon a time there was a rajah who had seven beautiful daughters. They were all good girls; but the youngest, named Balna, was more clever than the rest. The rajah's wife died when they were quite little children, so these seven poor princesses were left with no mother to take care of them.

The rajah's daughters took it by turns to cook their father's dinner every day, whilst he was absent deliberating with his Ministers on the affairs of the nation.

About this time the prudhan [prime minister] died, leaving a widow and one daughter; and every day, every day, when the seven princesses were preparing their father's dinner, the prudhan's widow and daughter would come and beg for a little fire from the hearth. Then Balna used to say to her sisters,

'Send that woman away; send her away. Let her get the fire at her own house. What does she want with ours? If we allow her to come here we shall suffer for it someday.'

But the other sisters would answer,

'Be quiet Balna; why must you always be quarrelling with this poor woman? Let her take some fire if she likes.'

Then the prudhan's widow used to go to the hearth and take a few sticks from it and whilst no one was looking, she would quickly throw some mud into the midst of the dishes which were being prepared for the rajah's dinner.

Now the rajah was very fond of his daughters. Ever since their mother's death they had cooked his dinner with their own hands, in order to avoid the danger of his being poisoned by his enemies. So, when he found the mud mixed up with his dinner, he thought it must arise from their carelessness, as it appeared improbable that anyone should have put mud there on purpose; but being very kind he did not like to reprove them for it, although this spoiling of the curry was repeated many successive days.

At last, one day, he determined to hide, and watch his daughters cooking, and see how it all happened; so he went into the next room, and watched them through a hole in the wall.

There he saw his seven daughters carefully washing the rice and preparing the curry, and as each dish was completed they put it by the fire ready to be cooked. Next he noticed the prudhan's widow come to the door, and beg for a few sticks from the fire to cook her dinner with. Balna turned to her angrily and said,

'Why don't you keep fuel in your own house, and not come here every day and take ours? – Sisters, don't give this woman any more wood; let her buy it for herself.'

Then the eldest sister answered,

'Balna, let the poor woman take the wood and the fire; she does us no harm.'

But Balna replied,

'If you let her come here so often, maybe she will do some harm, and make us sorry for it someday.'

The rajah then saw the prudhan's widow go to the place where all his dinner was nicely prepared, and, as she took the wood, she threw a little mud into each of the dishes.

At this he was very angry, and sent to have the woman seized and brought before him. But when the widow came, she told him she had played this trick because she wanted to gain an audience with him; and she spoke so cleverly, and pleased him so well with her cunning words, that instead of punishing her, the rajah married her, and made her his ranee, and she and her daughter came to live in the palace.

Now the new ranee hated the seven poor princesses, and wanted to get them, if possible, out of the way, in order that her daughter might have all their riches, and live in the palace as princess in their place; and instead of being grateful to them for their kindness to her she did all she could to make them miserable. She gave them nothing but bread to eat, and very little of that, and very little water to drink; so these seven poor little princesses, who had been accustomed to have everything comfortable about them, and good food and good clothes all their lives long, were very miserable and unhappy; and they used to go out every day and sit by their dead mother's tomb and cry – and say,

'Oh mother, mother! Cannot you see your poor children, how unhappy we are, and how we are starved by our cruel stepmother?'

One day, whilst they were thus sobbing and crying, lo and behold! A beautiful pomelo tree grew up out of the grave, covered with fresh ripe pomeloes, and the children satisfied their hunger by eating some of the fruit, and every day after this, instead of trying to eat the bad dinner their stepmother provided for them, they used to go out to their mother's grave and eat the pomeloes which grew there on the beautiful tree.

Then the ranee said to her daughter,

'I cannot tell how it is, every day those seven girls say they don't want any dinner, and won't eat any; and yet they never grow thin nor look ill; they look better than you do. I cannot tell how it is' – and she bade her watch the seven princesses, and see if anyone gave them anything to eat.

So next day when the princesses went to their mother's grave, and were eating the beautiful pomeloes, the prudhan's daughter followed them, and saw them gathering the fruit.

Then Balna said to her sisters,

'Do you not see that girl watching us? Let us drive her away, or hide the pomeloes, else she will go and tell her mother all about it, and that will be very bad for us.'

But the other sisters said,

'Oh no, do not be unkind, Balna. The girl would never be so cruel as to tell her mother. Let us rather invite her to come and have some of the fruit,' – and, calling her to them, they gave her one of the pomeloes.

No sooner had she eaten it, however, than the prudhan's daughter went home and said to her mother,

'I do not wonder the seven princesses will not eat the dinner you prepare for them, for by their mother's grave there grows a beautiful pomelo tree, and they go there every day and eat the pomeloes. I ate one, and it was the nicest I have ever tasted.'

The cruel ranee was much vexed at hearing this, and all next day she stayed in her room, and told the rajah that she had a very bad headache. The rajah was deeply grieved, and said to his wife,

'What can I do for you?'

She answered, 'There is only one thing that will make my headache well. By your dead wife's tomb there grows a fine pomelo tree; you must bring that here, and boil it, root and branch, and put a little of the water in which it has been boiled on my forehead, and that will cure my headache.'

So the rajah sent his servants, and had the beautiful pomelo tree pulled up by the roots, and did as the ranee desired; and when some of the water in which it had been boiled was put on her forehead, she said her headache was gone and she felt quite well.

Next day, when the seven princesses went as usual to the grave of their mother, the pomelo tree had disappeared. Then they all began to cry very bitterly.

Now there was by the ranee's tomb a small tank, and, as they were crying, they saw that the tank was filled with a rich cream-like substance, which quickly hardened into a thick white cake. At seeing this all the princesses were very glad, and they ate some of the cake, and liked it; and next day the same thing happened, and so it went on for many days. Every morning the princesses went to their mother's grave, and found the little tank filled with the nourishing cream-like cake.

Then the cruel stepmother said to her daughter,

'I cannot tell how it is, I have had the pomelo tree which used to grow by the ranee's grave destroyed, and yet the princesses grow no thinner, nor look more sad, though they never eat the dinner I give them. I cannot tell how it is!'

And her daughter said,

'I will watch.'

Next day while the princesses were eating the cream cake, who should come by but their stepmother's daughter! Balna saw her first, and said,

'See, sisters, there comes that girl again. Let us sit round the edge of the tank and not allow her to see it, for if we give her some of our cake, she will go and tell her mother; and that will be very unfortunate for us.'

The other sisters, however, thought Balna unnecessarily suspicious, and instead of following her advice, they gave the prudhan's daughter some of the cake, and she went home and told her mother all about it.

The ranee, on hearing how well the princesses fared, was exceedingly angry, and sent her servants to pull down the dead ranee's tomb, and fill the little tank with the ruins. And not content with this, she next day pretended to be very, very ill – in fact, at the point of death – and when the rajah was much grieved, and asked her whether it was in his power to procure her any remedy, she said to him,

'Only one thing can save my life, but I know you will not do it.'

He replied,

'Yes, whatever it is, I will do it.'

She then said,

'To save my life, you must kill the seven daughters of your first wife, and put some of their blood on my forehead and on the palms of my hands, and their death will be my life.'

At these words the rajah was very sorrowful; but because he feared to break his word, he went out with a heavy heart to find his daughters.

He found them crying by the ruins of their mother's grave.

Then, feeling he could not kill them, the rajah spoke kindly to them, and told them to come out into the jungle with him; and there he made a fire and cooked some rice, and gave it to them. But in the afternoon, it being very hot, the seven princesses all fell asleep, and when he saw they were fast asleep, the rajah, their father, stole away and left them saying to himself,

'It is better my poor daughters should die here, than be killed by their stepmother.'

He then shot a deer, and, returning home, put some of its blood on the forehead and hands of the ranee, and she thought then that he had really killed the princesses, and said she felt quite well.

Meantime the seven princesses awoke, and when they found themselves all alone in the thick jungle they were much frightened, and began to call out as loud as they could, in hopes of making their father hear; but he was by that time far away, and would not have been able to hear them even had their voices been as loud as thunder.

It so happened that this very day the seven young sons of a neighbouring rajah chanced to be hunting in that same jungle, and as they were returning home, after the day's sport was over, the youngest prince said to his brothers,

'Stop, I think I hear someone crying and calling out. Do you not hear voices? Let us go in the direction of the sound, and find out what it is.'

So the seven princes rode through the wood until they came to the place where the seven princesses sat crying and wringing their hands. At the sight of them the young princes were very much astonished, and still more so on learning their story: and they settled that each should take one of these poor forlorn ladies home with him, and marry her.

So the first and eldest prince took the eldest princess home with him, and married her;

And the second took the second;

And the third took the third;

And the fourth took the fourth;

And the fifth took the fifth;

And the sixth took the sixth;

And the seventh, and handsomest of all, took the beautiful Balna.

And when they got to their own land, there was great rejoicing throughout the kingdom, at the marriage of the seven young princes to seven such beautiful princesses.

About a year after this Balna had a little son, and his uncles and aunts were so fond of the boy that it was as if he had seven fathers and seven mothers. None of the other princes and princesses had any children, so the son of the seventh prince and Balna was acknowledged their heir by all the rest.

They had thus lived very happily for some time, when one fine day the seventh prince said he would go out hunting, and away he went; and they waited long for him, but he never came back.

Then his six brothers said they would go and see what had become of him; and they went away, but they also did not return.

And the seven princesses grieved very much, for they feared that their kind husbands must have been killed.

One day, not long after this happened, as Balna was rocking her baby's cradle, and whilst her sisters were working in the room below, there came to the palace door a man in a long black dress, who said that he was a fakir, and came to beg. The servants said to him,

'You cannot go into the palace – the rajah's sons have all gone away; we think they must be dead, and their widows cannot be interrupted by your begging.'

But he said,

'I am a holy man, you must let me in.'

Then the stupid servants let him walk through the palace, but they did not know that this was no fakir, but a wicked magician named Punchkin.

Punchkin fakir wandered through the palace, and saw many beautiful things there, till at last he reached the room where Balna sat singing beside her little boy's cradle. The magician thought her more beautiful than all the other beautiful things he had seen, insomuch, that he asked her to go home with him and to marry him. But she said,

'My husband, I fear, is dead, but my little boy is still quite young; I will stay here and teach him to grow up a clever man, and when he is grown up he shall go out into the world, and try and learn tidings of his father. Heaven forbid that I should ever leave him, or marry you!'

At these words the magician was very angry, and turned her into a little black dog, and led her away, saying,

'Since you will not come with me of your own free will, I will make you.'

So the poor princess was dragged away, without any power of effecting an escape, or of letting her sisters know what had become of her. As Punchkin passed through the palace gate the servants said to him,

'Where did you get that pretty little dog?'

And he answered,

'One of the princesses gave it to me as a present.'

At hearing which they let him go without further questioning.

Soon after this, the six elder princesses heard the little baby, their nephew, begin to cry, and when they went upstairs they were much surprised to find him all alone, and Balna nowhere to be seen. Then they questioned the servants, and when they heard of the fakir and the little black dog, they guessed what had happened, and sent in every direction seeking them, but neither the fakir nor the dog was to be found. What could six poor women do? They gave up all hopes of ever seeing their kind husbands, and their sister, and her husband, again, and devoted themselves thenceforward to teaching and taking care of their little nephew.

Thus time went on, till Balna's son was fourteen years old. Then, one day, his aunts told him the history of the family; and no sooner did he hear it, than he was seized with a great desire to go in search of his father and mother and uncles, and if he could find them alive to bring them home again. His aunts, on learning his determination, were much alarmed, and tried to dissuade him, saying,

'We have lost our husbands, and our sister, and her husband, and you are now our sole hope; if you go away, what shall we do?'

But he replied,

'I pray you not to be discouraged; I will return soon, and if it is possible bring my father and mother and uncles with me.'

So he set out on his travels; but for some months he could learn nothing to help him in his search.

At last, after he had journeyed many hundreds of weary miles, and become almost hopeless of ever hearing anything further of his parents, he one day came to a country that seemed full of stones, and rocks, and trees, and there he saw a large palace, with a high tower, hard by which was a malee's little house.

As he was looking about, the malee's wife saw him, and ran out of the house and said,

'My dear boy, who are you that dare venture to this dangerous place?'

He answered,

'I am a rajah's son, and I come in search of my father, and my uncles, and my mother whom a wicked enchanter bewitched.'

Then the malee's wife said,

'This country and this palace belong to a great enchanter; he is all-powerful, and if anyone displeases him, he can turn them into stones and trees. All the rocks and trees you see here were living people once, and the magician turned them to what they now are. Some time ago a rajah's son came here, and shortly afterwards came his six brothers, and they were all turned into stones and trees; and these are not the only unfortunate ones, for up in that tower lives a beautiful princess, whom the magician has kept prisoner there for twelve years, because she hates him and will not marry him.'

Then the little prince thought,

'These must be my parents and my uncles. I have found what I seek at last.'

So he told his story to the malee's wife, and begged her to help him to remain in that place a while and inquire further concerning tile unhappy people she mentioned; and she promised to befriend him, and advised his disguising himself lest the magician should see him, and turn him likewise into stone. To this the prince agreed. So the malee's wife dressed him up in a saree, and pretended that he was her daughter.

One day, not long after this, as the magician was walking in his garden, he saw the little girl playing about, and asked her who she was. She told him she was the malee's daughter, and the magician said,

'You are a pretty little girl, and tomorrow you shall take a present of flowers from me to the beautiful lady who lives in the tower.'

The young prince was much delighted at hearing this, and went immediately to inform the malee's wife; after consultation with whom he determined that it would be more safe for him to retain his disguise, and trust to the chance of a favourable opportunity for establishing some communication with his mother, if it were indeed she.

Now it happened that at Balna's marriage her husband had given her a small gold ring on which her name was engraved, and she had put it on her little son's finger when he was a baby, and afterwards when he was older his aunts had had it enlarged for him, so that he was still able to wear it. The malee's wife advised him to fasten the well-known treasure to one of the bouquets he presented to his mother, and trust to her recognizing it.

This was not to be done without difficulty, as such a strict watch was kept over the poor princess, for fear of her ever establishing communication with her friends, that though the supposed malee's daughter was permitted to take her flowers every day, the magician or one of his slaves was always in the room at the time.

At last, one day, however, opportunity favoured him, and when no one was looking, the boy tied the ring to a nosegay, and threw it at Balna's feet. It fell with a clang on the floor, and Balna, looking to see what made the strange sound, found the little ring tied to the flowers.

On recognizing it, she at once believed the story her son told her of his long search, and begged him to advise her as to what she had better do; at the same time entreating him on no account to endanger his life by trying to rescue her. She told him that, for twelve long years, the magician had kept her shut up in the tower because she refused to marry him, and she was so closely guarded that she saw no hope of release.

Now Balna's son was a bright, clever boy, so he said,

'Do not fear, dear mother; the first thing to do is to discover how far the magician's power extends, in order that we may be able to liberate my father and uncles, whom he has imprisoned in the form of rocks and trees. You have spoken to him angrily for twelve long years; now rather speak kindly. Tell him you have given up all hopes of again seeing the husband you have so long mourned; and say you are willing to marry him. Then endeavour to find out what his power consists in, and whether he is immortal, or can be put to death.'

Balna determined to take her son's advice, and the next day sent for Punchkin, and spoke to him as had been suggested.

The magician, greatly delighted, begged her to allow the wedding to take place as soon as possible.

But she told him that before she married him he must allow her a little more time, in which she might make his acquaintance – and that, after being enemies so long, their friendship could but strengthen by degrees.

'And do tell me,' she said, 'are you quite immortal? Can death never touch you? And are you too great an enchanter ever to feel human suffering?'

'Why do you ask?' said he.

'Because,' she replied, 'if I am to be your wife, I would fain know all about you, in order, if any calamity threatens you, to overcome, or if possible to avert it.'

'It is true,' he said, 'that I am not as others. Far, far away, hundreds of thousands of miles from this, there lies a desolate country covered with thick jungle. In the midst of the jungle grows a circle of palm trees, and in the centre of the circle stand six chattees full of water, piled one above another: below the sixth chattee is a small cage which contains a little green parrot – on the life of the parrot depends my life – and if the parrot is killed I must die. It is, however,' he added, 'impossible that the parrot should sustain any injury, both on account of the inaccessibility of the country, and because, by my appointment, many thousand jinn surround the palm trees, and kill all who approach the place.'

Balna told her son what Punchkin had said; but at the same time implored him to give up all idea of getting the parrot.

The prince, however, replied,

'Mother, unless I can get hold of that parrot, you, and my father, and uncles, cannot be liberated; be not afraid, I will shortly return. Do you, meantime, keep the magician in good humour – still putting off your marriage with him on various pretexts; and before he finds out the cause of delay, I will be here.'

So saying, he went away.

Many, many weary miles did he travel, till at last he came to a thick jungle; and, being very tired, sat down under a tree and fell asleep. He was awakened by a soft rustling sound; and looking about him, saw a large serpent which was making its way to an eagle's nest built in the tree under which he lay; and in the nest were two young eagles. The prince seeing the danger of the young birds, drew his sword, and killed the serpent; at the same moment a rushing sound was heard in the air, and the two old eagles, who had been out hunting for food for their young ones, returned. They quickly saw the dead serpent and the young prince standing over it; and the old mother eagle said to him,

'Dear boy, for many years all our young ones have been devoured by that cruel serpent: you have now saved the lives of our children; whenever you are in need, therefore, send to us and we will help you; and as for these little eagles, take them, and let them be your servants.'

At this the prince was very glad, and the two eaglets crossed their wings, on which he mounted; and they carried him far, far away over the thick jungles, until he came to the place where grew the circle of palm trees: in the midst of which stood the six chattees full of water.

It was the middle of the day, and the heat was very great. All around the trees were the jinn, fast asleep: nevertheless, there were such countless thousands of them, that it would have been quite impossible for anyone to walk through their ranks to the place; down swooped the strong-winged eaglets – down jumped the prince: in an instant he had overthrown the six chattees full of water, and seized the little green parrot, which he rolled up in his cloak; while, as he mounted again into the air, all the jinn below awoke, and finding their treasure gone, set up a wild and melancholy howl.

Away, away flew the little eagles, till they came to their home in the great tree; then the prince said to the old eagles,

'Take back your little ones; they have done me good service; if ever again I stand in need of help, I will not fail to come to you.'

He then continued his journey on foot till he arrived once more at the magician's palace; where he sat down at the door and began playing with the parrot. Punchkin saw him, and came to him quickly, and said,

'My boy, where did you get that parrot? Give it to me, I pray you.'

But the prince answered,

'Oh no, I cannot give away my parrot, it is a great pet of mine; I have had it many years.'

Then the magician said,

'If it is an old favourite, I can understand your not caring to give it away – but come, what will you sell it for?'

'Sir,' replied the prince, 'I will not sell my parrot.'

Then Punchkin got frightened, and said,

Anything, anything; name what price you will, and it shall be yours.'

The prince answered,

'Let the seven rajah's sons whom you turned into rocks and trees be instantly liberated.'

'It is done as you desire,' said the magician, 'only give me my parrot.'

And with that, by a stroke of his wand, Balna's husband and his brothers resumed their natural shapes.

'Now give me my parrot,' repeated Punchkin.

'Not so fast, my master,' rejoined the prince, 'I must first beg that you will restore to life all whom you have thus imprisoned.'

The magician immediately waved his wand again; and whilst he cried, in an imploring voice,

'Give me my parrot!'

The whole garden became suddenly alive: where rocks, and stones, and trees had been before, stood rajah's, and punts, and sirdars, and mighty men on prancing horses, and jewelled pages, and troops of armed attendants.

'Give me my parrot!' cried Punchkin.

Then the boy took hold of the parrot, and tore off one of his wings; and as he did so the magician's right arm fell off.

Punchkin then stretched out his left arm, crying,

'Give me my parrot!'

The prince pulled off the parrot's second wing, and the magician's left arm tumbled off.

'Give me my parrot!' cried he, and fell on his knees.

The prince pulled off the parrot's right leg, the magician's right leg fell off: the prince pulled off the parrot's left leg, down fell the magician's left.

Nothing remained of him save the limbless body and the head; but still he rolled his eyes, and cried,

'Give me my parrot!'

'Take your parrot, then,' cried the boy, and with that he wrung the bird's neck, and threw it at the magician; and, as he did so, Punchkin's head twisted round, and, with a fearful groan, he died!

Then they let Balna out of the tower; and she, her son, and the seven princes went to their own country, and lived very happily ever afterwards.

And as to the rest of the world, everyone went to his own house.

From: Old Deccan Days

Judgements of Karakash

A WEAVER, CLOSING his shop for the night, left a long needle sticking in his work on the loom. A thief got in with a false key, and, as he was stumbling about in the dark, the needle put out one of his eyes. In great pain, he slipped back out, locking the door behind him.

Next morning, the injured thief told his story to Karakash, the impartial judge, who at once sent for the weaver, and regarding him sternly, asked,

'Did you leave a packing needle in the cloth on your loom when you shut your shop last night?'

'Yes.'

'Well, this poor thief has lost his eye through your carelessness; he was going to rob your shop; he stumbled, and the needle pierced his eye. Am I not Karakash, the impartial judge? This poor thief has lost an eye through your fault; so you shall lose an eye in like manner.'

'But, my lord,' said the weaver, 'he came to rob me; he had no right there.'

'We are not concerned with what this robber came to do, but with what he did. Was your shop-door broken open or damaged this morning; or was anything missing?'

'No.'

'He has done you no harm then, and you do but add insult to injury by throwing up his way of life against him. Justice demands that you lose an eye.'

The weaver offered money to the robber, to the judge, but in vain; the impartial judge would not be moved.

At last, a bright thought struck him, and he said,

'An eye for an eye is justice, O my lord the judge; yet in this case it is not quite fair on me. You are the impartial judge, and I submit to you that I, being a married man with children, shall suffer more damage in the loss of an eye than this poor robber, who has no one dependent on him. How could I go on weaving with but one eye? But I have a good neighbour, a gunsmith, who is a single man. Let one of his eyes be put out. What does he want with two eyes, for looking along gun barrels?'

The impartial judge, struck with the justice of these arguments, sent for the gunsmith, and had his eye put out.

A carpenter was fitting the doors and lattice-work to a house newly built, when a stone over a window fell and broke one of his legs. He complained to Karakash, the impartial judge, who called the lord of the house, and charged him with culpable negligence.

'It is not my fault, but the builder's,' pleaded the lord of the house; so the builder was sent for.

The builder said that it was not his fault, because at the moment he was laying that particular stone a girl passed by in a dress of so bright a red that he could not see what he was doing.

The impartial judge caused search to be made for that girl.

She was found, and brought before him.

'O veiled one,' he said, 'the red dress which you wore on such a day has cost this carpenter a broken leg, and so you must pay the damages.'

'It was not my fault, but the draper's,' said the girl.

'Because when I went to buy stuff for a dress, he had none but that particular bright red.'

The draper was forthwith summoned. He said it was not his fault, because the English manufacturer had sent him only this bright red material, though he had ordered others.

'What! You dog!' cried Karakash, 'Do you deal with the heathen?' and he ordered the draper to be hanged from the lintel of his own door.

The servants of justice took him and were going to hang him, but he was a tall man and the door of his house was low; so they returned to the judge, who inquired,

'Is the dog dead?'

They replied,

'He is tall, and the door of his house is very low. He will not hang there.'

'Then hang the first short man you can find,' said Karakash.

A certain rich old miser was subject to fainting fits, which tantalized two nephews who desired his death; for, though constantly falling down lifeless, he always got up again. Unable to bear the strain any longer, they took him in one of his fits and prepared him for burial.

They called in the professional layer-out, who took off the miser's clothes which, by ancient custom, were his perquisite, bound up his jaws, performed the usual ablutions upon the body, stuffed the nostrils, ears and other apertures with cotton wool against the entrance of demons, sprinkled the wool with a mixture of water, pounded camphor, and dried and pounded leaves of the lotus tree, and also with rosewater; bound the feet together by a bandage round the ankles, and disposed the hands upon the breast.

All this took time, and before the operator had quite finished, the miser revived; but he was so frightened at what was going on, that he fainted again; and his nephews were able to get the funeral procession underway.

They had performed half the road to the cemetery when the miser was again brought to life by the jolting of the bier, caused by the constant change of the bearers, who incessantly pressed forward to relieve one another in the meritorious act of carrying a true believer to the grave.

Lifting the loose lid, he sat up, and roared for help.

To his relief he saw Karakash, the impartial judge, coming down the path the procession was mounting, and appealed to him by name.

The judge at once stopped the procession, and, confronting the nephews, asked,

'Is your uncle dead or alive?'

'Quite dead, my lord.'

He turned to the hired mourners.

'Is this corpse dead or alive?'

'Quite dead, my lord,' came the answer from a hundred throats.

'But you can see for yourself that I am alive!' cried the miser wildly.

Karakash looked him sternly in both eyes.

'Allah forbid,' said he, 'that I should allow the evidence of my poor senses, and your bare word, to weigh against this crowd of witnesses. Am I not the impartial judge? Proceed with the funeral!'

At this the old man once more fainted away, and in that state was peacefully buried.

From: Folklore of the Holy Land

The Story of Pretty Goldilocks

Once upon a time there was a princess who was the prettiest creature in the world.

And because she was so beautiful, and because her hair was like the finest gold, and waved and rippled nearly to the ground, she was called Pretty Goldilocks. She always wore a crown of flowers, and her dresses were embroidered with diamonds and pearls, and everybody who saw her fell in love with her.

Now one of her neighbours was a young king who was not married.

He was very rich and handsome, and when he heard all that was said about Pretty Goldilocks, though he had never seen her, he fell so deeply in love with her that he could neither eat nor drink. So he resolved to send an ambassador to ask her in marriage. He had a splendid carriage made for his ambassador, and gave him more than a hundred horses and a hundred servants, and told him to be sure and bring the princess back with him.

After he had started nothing else was talked of at Court, and the king felt so sure that the princess would consent that he set his people to work at pretty dresses and splendid furniture, that they might be ready by the time she came.

Meanwhile, the ambassador arrived at the princess's palace and delivered his little message, but whether she happened to be cross that day, or whether the compliment did not please her, is not known. She only answered that she was very much obliged to the king, but she had no wish to be married.

The ambassador set off sadly on his homeward way, bringing all the king's presents back with him, for the princess was too well brought up to accept the pearls and diamonds when she would not accept the king, so she had only kept twenty-five English pins that he might not be vexed.

When the ambassador reached the city, where the king was waiting impatiently, everybody was very much annoyed with him for not bringing the princess, and the king cried like a baby, and nobody could console him.

Now there was at the Court a young man, who was more clever and handsome than anyone else. He was called Charming, and everyone loved him, excepting a few envious people who were angry at his being the king's favourite and knowing all the State secrets. He happened to one day be with some people who were speaking of the ambassador's return and saying that his going to the princess had not done much good, when Charming said rashly,

'If the king had sent me to the princess Goldilocks I am sure she would have come back with me.'

His enemies at once went to the king and said,

'You will hardly believe, sire, what Charming has the audacity to say – that if he had been sent to the princess Goldilocks she would certainly have come back with him. He seems to think that he is so much handsomer than you that the princess would have fallen in love with him and followed him willingly.'

The king was very angry when he heard this.

'Ha, ha!' said he; 'does he laugh at my unhappiness, and think himself more fascinating than I am? Go, and let him be shut up in my great tower to die of hunger.'

So the king's guards went to fetch Charming, who had thought no more of his rash speech, and carried him off to prison with great cruelty. The poor prisoner had only a little straw for his bed, and but for a little stream of water which flowed through the tower he would have died of thirst.

One day when he was in despair he said to himself,

'How can I have offended the king? I am his most faithful subject, and have done nothing against him.'

The king chanced to be passing the tower and recognized the voice of his former favourite. He stopped to listen in spite of Charming's enemies, who tried to persuade him to have nothing more to do with the traitor. But the king said,

'Be quiet, I wish to hear what he says.'

And then he opened the tower door and called to Charming, who came very sadly and kissed the king's hand, saying,

'What have I done, sire, to deserve this cruel treatment?'

'You mocked me and my ambassador,' said the king, 'and you said that if I had sent you for the princess Goldilocks you would certainly have brought her back.'

'It is quite true, sire,' replied Charming;

'I should have drawn such a picture of you, and represented your good qualities in such a way, that I am certain the princess would have found you irresistible. But I cannot see what there is in that to make you angry.'

The king could not see any cause for anger either when the matter was presented to him in this light, and he began to frown very fiercely at the courtiers who had so misrepresented his favourite.

So he took Charming back to the palace with him, and after seeing that he had a very good supper he said to him,

'You know that I love Pretty Goldilocks as much as ever, her refusal has not made any difference to me; but I don't know how to make her change her mind; I really should like to send you, to see if you can persuade her to marry me.'

Charming replied that he was perfectly willing to go, and would set out the very next day.

'But you must wait till I can get a grand escort for you,' said the king.

But Charming said that he only wanted a good horse to ride, and the king, who was delighted at his being ready to start so promptly, gave him letters to the princess, and bade him good speed.

It was on a Monday morning that he set out all alone upon his errand, thinking of nothing but how he could persuade the princess Goldilocks to marry the king. He had a writing-book in his pocket, and whenever any happy thought struck him he dismounted from his horse and sat down under the trees to put it into the harangue which he was preparing for the princess, before he forgot it.

One day when he had started at the very earliest dawn, and was riding over a great meadow, he suddenly had a capital idea, and, springing from his horse, he sat down under a willow tree which grew by a little river.

When he had written it down he was looking around him, pleased to find himself in such a pretty place, when all at once he saw a great golden carp lying gasping and exhausted upon the grass. In leaping after little flies she had thrown herself high upon the bank, where she had lain till she was nearly dead.

Charming had pity upon her, and, though he couldn't help thinking that she would have been very nice for dinner, he picked her up gently and put her back into the water. As soon as Dame Carp felt the refreshing coolness of the water she sank down joyfully to the bottom of the river, then, swimming up to the bank quite boldly, she said,

'I thank you, Charming, for the kindness you have done me. You have saved my life; one day I will repay you.'

So saying, she sank down into the water again, leaving Charming greatly astonished at her politeness.

Another day, as he journeyed on, he saw a raven in great distress. The poor bird was closely pursued by an eagle, which would soon have eaten it up, had not Charming quickly fitted an arrow to his bow and shot the eagle dead.

The raven perched upon a tree very joyfully.

'Charming,' said he, 'it was very generous of you to rescue a poor raven; I am not ungrateful, someday I will repay you.'

Charming thought it was very nice of the raven to say so, and went on his way.

Before the sun rose he found himself in a thick wood where it was too dark for him to see his path, and here he heard an owl crying as if it were in despair.

'Hark!' said he, 'that must be an owl in great trouble, I am sure it has gone into a snare'; and he began to hunt about, and presently found a great net which some bird-catchers had spread the night before.

'What a pity it is that men do nothing but torment and persecute poor creatures which never do them any harm!' said he, and he took out his knife and cut the cords of the net, and the owl flitted away into the darkness, but then turning, with one flicker of her wings, she came back to Charming and said,

'It does not need many words to tell you how great a service you have done me. I was caught; in a few minutes the fowlers would have been here – without your help I should have been killed. I am grateful, and one day I will repay you.'

These three adventures were the only ones of any consequence that befell Charming upon his journey, and he made all the haste he could to reach the palace of the princess Goldilocks.

When he arrived he thought everything he saw delightful and magnificent. Diamonds were as plentiful as pebbles, and the gold and silver, the beautiful dresses, the sweetmeats and pretty things that were everywhere quite amazed him; he thought to himself,

'If the princess consents to leave all this, and come with me to marry the king, he may think himself lucky!'

Then he dressed himself carefully in rich brocade, with scarlet and white plumes, and threw a splendid embroidered scarf over his shoulder, and, looking as graceful as possible, he presented himself at the door of the palace, carrying in his arm a tiny pretty dog which he had bought on the way.

The guards saluted him respectfully, and a messenger was sent to the princess to announce the arrival of Charming as ambassador of her neighbour the king.

'Charming,' said the princess, 'the name promises well; I have no doubt that he is good-looking and fascinates everybody.'

'Indeed he does, madam,' said all her maids of honour in one breath. 'We saw him from the window of the garret where we were spinning flax, and we could do nothing but look at him as long as he was in sight.'

'Well to be sure,' said the princess, 'that's how you amuse yourselves, is it? Looking at strangers out of the window! Be quick and give me my blue satin embroidered dress, and comb out my golden hair. Let somebody make me fresh garlands of flowers, and give me my high-heeled shoes and my fan, and tell them to sweep my great hall and my throne, for I want everyone to say I am really 'Pretty Goldilocks'.'

You can imagine how all her maids scurried this way and that to make the princess ready, and how in their haste they knocked their heads together and hindered each other, till she thought they would never have done.

However, at last they led her into the gallery of mirrors that she might assure herself that nothing was lacking in her appearance, and then she mounted her throne of gold, ebony, and ivory, while her ladies took their guitars and began to sing softly. Then Charming was led in, and was so struck with astonishment and admiration that at first not a word could he say. But presently he took courage and delivered his harangue, bravely ending by begging the princess to spare him the disappointment of going back without her.

'Sir Charming,' answered she, 'all the reasons you have given me are very good ones, and I assure you that I should have more pleasure in obliging you than anyone else, but you must know that a month ago as I was walking by the river with my ladies I took off my glove, and as I did so a ring that I was wearing slipped off my finger and rolled into the water. As I valued it more than my kingdom, you may imagine how vexed I was at losing it, and I vowed to never listen to any proposal of marriage unless the ambassador first brought me back my ring. So now you know what is expected of you, for if you talked for fifteen days and fifteen nights you could not make me change my mind.'

Charming was very much surprised by this answer, but he bowed low to the princess, and begged her to accept the embroidered scarf and the tiny dog he had brought with him. But she answered that she did not want any presents, and that he was to remember what she had just told him.

When he got back to his lodging he went to bed without eating any supper, and his little dog, who was called Frisk, couldn't eat any either, but came and lay down close to him. All night Charming sighed and lamented.

'How am I to find a ring that fell into the river a month ago?' said he.

'It is useless to try; the princess must have told me to do it on purpose, knowing it was impossible.'

And then he sighed again.

Frisk heard him and said,

'My dear master, don't despair; the luck may change, you are too good not to be happy. Let us go down to the river as soon as it is light.'

But Charming only gave him two little pats and said nothing, and very soon he fell asleep.

At the first glimmer of dawn Frisk began to jump about, and when he had waked Charming they went out together, first into the garden, and then down to the river's brink, where they wandered up and down. Charming was thinking sadly of having to go back unsuccessful when he heard someone calling,

'Charming, Charming!'

He looked all about him and thought he must be dreaming, as he could not see anybody. Then he walked on and the voice called again,

'Charming, Charming!'

'Who calls me?' said he. Frisk, who was very small and could look closely into the water, cried out,

'I see a golden carp coming.'

And sure enough there was the great carp, who said to Charming,

'You saved my life in the meadow by the willow tree, and I promised that I would repay you. Take this, it is princess Goldilock's ring.'

Charming took the ring out of Dame Carp's mouth, thanking her a thousand times, and he and tiny Frisk went straight to the palace, where someone told the princess that he was asking to see her.

'Ah! Poor fellow,' said she, 'he must have come to say goodbye, finding it impossible to do as I asked.'

So in came Charming, who presented her with the ring and said,

'Madam, I have done your bidding. Will it please you to marry my master?'

When the princess saw her ring brought back to her unhurt she was so astonished that she thought she must be dreaming.

'Truly, Charming,' said she, 'you must be the favourite of some fairy, or you could never have found it.'

'Madam,' answered he, 'I was helped by nothing but my desire to obey your wishes.'

'Since you are so kind,' said she, 'perhaps you will do me another service, for till it is done I will never be married. There is a prince not far from here whose name is Galifron, who once wanted to marry me, but when I refused he uttered the most terrible threats against me, and vowed that he would lay waste my country. But what could I do? I could not marry a frightful giant as tall as a tower, who eats up people as a monkey eats chestnuts, and who talks so loud that anybody who has to listen to him becomes quite deaf. Nevertheless, he does not cease to persecute me and to kill my subjects. So before I can listen to your proposal you must kill him and bring me his head.'

Charming was rather dismayed at this command, but he answered,

'Very well, princess, I will fight this Galifron; I believe that he will kill me, but at any rate I shall die in your defence.'

Then the princess was frightened and said everything she could think of to prevent Charming from fighting the giant, but it was of no use, and he went out to arm himself suitably, and then, taking little Frisk with him, he mounted his horse and set out for Galifron's country. Everyone he met told him what a terrible giant Galifron was, and that nobody dared go near him; and the more he heard, the more frightened he grew. Frisk tried to encourage him by saying,

'While you are fighting the giant, dear master, I will go and bite his heels, and when he stoops down to look at me you can kill him.'

Charming praised his little dog's plan, but knew that this help would not do much good.

At last he drew near the giant's castle, and saw to his horror that every path that led to it was strewn with bones. Before long he saw Galifron coming. His head was higher than the tallest trees, and he sang in a terrible voice,

'Bring out your little boys and girls,
'Pray do not stay to do their curls,
'For I shall eat so very many,
'I shall not know if they have any.'

Thereupon Charming sang out as loud as he could to the same tune,

'Come out and meet the valiant Charming
'Who finds you not at all alarming;
'Although he is not very tall,
'He's big enough to make you fall.'

The rhymes were not very correct, but you see he had made them up so quickly that it is a miracle that they were not worse; especially as he was horribly frightened all the time.

When Galifron heard these words he looked all about him, and saw Charming standing, sword in hand this put the giant into a terrible rage, and he aimed a blow at Charming with his huge iron club, which would certainly have killed him if it had reached him, but at that instant a raven perched upon the giant's head, and, pecking with its strong beak and beating with its great wings so confused and blinded him that all his blows fell harmlessly upon the air, and Charming, rushing in, gave him several strokes with his sharp sword so that he fell to the ground.

Whereupon Charming cut off his head before he knew anything about it, and the raven from a tree close by croaked out,

'You see I have not forgotten the good turn you did me in killing the eagle. Today I think I have fulfilled my promise of repaying you.'

'Indeed, I owe you more gratitude than you ever owed me,' replied Charming. And then he mounted his horse and rode off with Galifron's head.

When he reached the city the people ran after him in crowds, crying,

'Behold the brave Charming, who has killed the giant!'

And their shouts reached the princess's ear, but she dared not ask what was happening, for fear she should hear that Charming had been killed.

But very soon he arrived at the palace with the giant's head, of which she was still terrified, though it could no longer do her any harm.

'Princess,' said Charming, 'I have killed your enemy; I hope you will now consent to marry the king my master.'

'Oh dear! no,' said the princess, 'not until you have brought me some water from the Gloomy Cavern.

'Not far from here there is a deep cave, the entrance to which is guarded by two dragons with fiery eyes, who will not allow anyone to pass them. When you get into the cavern you will find an immense hole, which you must go down, and it is full of toads and snakes; at the bottom of this hole there is another little cave, in which rises the Fountain of Health and Beauty. It is some of this water that I really must have: everything it touches becomes wonderful. The beautiful things will always remain beautiful, and the ugly things become lovely. If one is young one never grows old, and if one is old one becomes young. You see, Charming, I could not leave my kingdom without taking some of it with me.'

'Princess,' said he, 'you at least can never need this water, but I am an unhappy ambassador, whose death you desire. Where you send me I will go, though I know I shall never return.'

And, as the princess Goldilocks showed no sign of relenting, he started with his little dog for the Gloomy Cavern. Everyone he met on the way said,

'What a pity that a handsome young man should throw away his life so carelessly! He is going to the cavern alone, though if he had a hundred men with him he could not succeed. Why does the princess ask impossibilities?'

Charming said nothing, but he was very sad. When he was near the top of a hill he dismounted to let his horse graze, while Frisk amused himself by chasing flies. Charming knew he could not be far from the Gloomy Cavern, and on looking about him he saw a black hideous rock from which came a thick smoke, followed in a moment by one of the dragons with fire blazing from his mouth and eyes.

His body was yellow and green, and his claws scarlet, and his tail was so long that it lay in a hundred coils. Frisk was so terrified at the sight of it that he did not know where to hide. Charming, quite determined to get the water or die, now drew his sword, and, taking the crystal flask which Pretty Goldilocks had given him to fill, said to Frisk,

'I feel sure that I shall never come back from this expedition; when I am dead, go to the princess and tell her that her errand has cost me my life. Then find the king my master, and relate all my adventures to him.'

As he spoke he heard a voice calling,

'Charming, Charming!'

'Who calls me?' said he; then he saw an owl sitting in a hollow tree, who said to him,

'You saved my life when I was caught in the net, now I can repay you. Trust me with the flask, for I know all the ways of the Gloomy Cavern, and can fill it from the Fountain of Beauty.'

Charming was only too glad to give her the flask, and she flitted into the cavern quite unnoticed by the dragon, and after some time returned with the flask, filled to the very brim with sparkling water. Charming thanked her with all his heart, and joyfully hastened back to the town.

He went straight to the palace and gave the flask to the princess, who had no further objection to make. So she thanked Charming, and ordered that preparations should be made for her departure, and they soon set out together. The princess found Charming such an agreeable companion that she sometimes said to him,

'Why didn't we stay where we were? I could have made you king, and we should have been so happy!'

But Charming only answered,

'I could not have done anything that would have vexed my master so much, even for a kingdom, or to please you, though I think you are as beautiful as the sun.'

At last they reached the king's great city, and he came out to meet the princess, bringing magnificent presents, and the marriage was celebrated with great rejoicings. But Goldilocks was so fond of Charming that she could not be happy unless he was near her, and she was always singing his praises.

'If it hadn't been for Charming,' she said to the king, 'I should never have come here; you ought to be very much obliged to him, for he did the most impossible things and got me water from the Fountain of Beauty, so I can never grow old, and shall get prettier every year.'

Then Charming's enemies said to the king,

'It is a wonder that you are not jealous, the queen thinks there is nobody in the world like Charming. As if anybody you had sent could not have done just as much!'

'It is quite true, now I come to think of it,' said the king. 'Let him be chained hand and foot, and thrown into the tower.'

So they took Charming, and as a reward for having served the king so faithfully he was shut up in the tower, where he only saw the jailer, who brought him a piece of black bread and a pitcher of water every day.

However, little Frisk came to console him, and told him all the news.

When Pretty Goldilocks heard what had happened she threw herself at the king's feet and begged him to set Charming free, but the more she cried, the more angry he was, and at last she saw that it was useless to say any more; but it made her very sad.

Then the king took it into his head that perhaps he was not handsome enough to please the princess Goldilocks, and he thought he would bathe his face with the water from the Fountain of Beauty, which was in the flask on a shelf in the princess's room, where she had placed it that she might see it often.

Now it happened that one of the princess's ladies in chasing a spider had knocked the flask off the shelf and broken it, and every drop of the water had been spilt. Not knowing what to do, she had hastily swept away the pieces of crystal, and then remembered that in the king's room she had seen a flask of exactly the same shape, also filled with sparkling water.

So, without saying a word, she fetched it and stood it upon the Queen's shelf.

Now the water in this flask was what was used in the kingdom for getting rid of troublesome people. Instead of having their heads cut off in the usual way, their faces were bathed with the water, and they instantly fell asleep and never woke up any more. So, when the king, thinking to improve his beauty, took the flask and sprinkled the water upon his face, *he* fell asleep, and nobody could wake him.

Little Frisk was the first to hear the news, and he ran to tell Charming, who sent him to beg the princess not to forget the poor prisoner. All the palace was in confusion on account of the king's death, but tiny Frisk made his way through the crowd to the princess's side, and said,

'Madam, do not forget poor Charming.'

Then she remembered all he had done for her, and without saying a word to anyone went straight to the tower, and with her own hands took off Charming's chains. Then, putting a golden crown upon his head, and the royal mantle upon his shoulders, she said,

'Come, faithful Charming, I make you king, and will take you for my husband.'

Charming, once more free and happy, fell at her feet and thanked her for her gracious words.

Everybody was delighted that he should be king, and the wedding, which took place at once, was the prettiest that can be imagined, and Prince Charming and Princess Goldilocks lived happily ever after.

From: The Blue Fairy Book

The Hero Twins

Maw-Sahv and Oo-yah-wee, as the Hero Twins are named in Queres, had the Sun for a father. Their mother died when they were born, and lay lifeless upon the hot plain. But the two wonderful boys, as soon as they were a minute old, were big and strong, and began playing.

There chanced to be in a cliff to the southward a nest of white crows; and presently the young crows said,

'Nana, what is that over there? Isn't it two babies?'

'Yes,' replied the Mother-Crow, when she had taken a look. 'Wait and I will bring them.'

So she brought the boys safely, and then their dead mother; and, rubbing a magic herb on the body of the latter, soon brought her to life.

By this time Maw-Sahv and Oo-yah-wee were sizable boys, and the mother started homeward with them.

'Now,' said she when they reached the edge of the valley and could look across to that wondrous rock whereon stands Acoma, 'go to yonder town, my sons, for that is where live your grandfather and grandmother, my parents; and I will wait here. Go ye in at the west end of the town and stand at the south end of the council grounds until someone speaks to you; and ask them to take you to the

Cacique, for he is your grandfather. You will know his house, for the ladder to it has three uprights instead of two. When you go in and tell your story, he will ask you a question to see if you are really his grandchildren, and will give you four chances to answer what he has in a bag in the corner. No one has ever been able to guess what is in it, but there are birds.'

The Twins did as they were bidden, and presently came to Acoma and found the house of the old Cacique. When they entered and told their story, he said,

'Now I will try you. What is in yonder bag?'

'A rattlesnake,' said the boys.

'No,' said the Cacique, 'it is not a rattlesnake. Try again.'

'Birds,' said the boys.

'Yes, they are birds. Now I know that you are truly my grandchildren, for no one else could ever guess.'

And he welcomed them gladly, and sent them back with new dresses and jewellery to bring their mother.

When she was about to arrive, the Twins ran ahead to the house and told her father, mother, and sister to leave the house until she should enter; but not knowing what was to come, they would not go out. When she had climbed the big ladder to the roof and started down through the trap door by the room-ladder, her sister cried out with joy at seeing her, and she was so startled that she fell from the ladder and broke her neck, and never could be brought to life again.

Maw-Sahv and Oo-yah-wee grew up to astounding adventures and achievements. While still very young in years, they did very remarkable things; for they had a miraculously rapid growth, and at an age when other boys were toddling about home, these Hero Twins had already become very famous hunters and warriors.

They were very fond of stories of adventure, like less precocious lads; and after the death of their mother they kept their grandmother busy telling them strange tales. She had a great many anecdotes of a certain ogre-giantess who lived in the dark gorges of the mountains to the South, and so much did Maw-Sahv and Oo-yah-wee hear of this wonderful personage – who was the terror of all that country – that their boyish ambition was fired.

One day when their grandmother was busy they stole away from home with their bows and arrows, and walked miles and miles, till they came to a great forest at the foot of the mountain. In the edge of it sat the old giant-woman, dozing in the sun, with a huge basket beside her. She was so enormous and looked so fierce that the boys' hearts stood still, and they would have hidden, but just then she caught sight of them, and called,

'Come, little boys, and get into this basket of mine, and I will take you to my house.'

'Very well,' said Maw-Sahv, bravely hiding his alarm. 'If you will take us through this big forest, which we would like to see, we will go with you.'

The giant-woman promised, and the lads clambered into her basket, which she took upon her back and started off. As she passed through the woods, the boys grabbed lumps of pitch from the tall pines and smeared it all over her head and back so softly that she did not notice it.

Once she sat down to rest, and the boys slyly put a lot of big stones in the basket, set fire to her pitched hair, and hurriedly climbed a tall pine.

Presently the giant-woman got up and started on toward home; but in a minute or two her head and manta were all of a blaze. With a howl that shook the earth, she dropped the basket and rolled on the ground, grinding her great head into the sand until she at last got the fire extinguished.

But she was badly scorched and very angry, and still angrier when she looked in the basket and found only a lot of stones. She retraced her steps until she found the boys hidden in the pine tree, and said to them,

'Come down, children, and get into my basket, that I may take you to my house, for now we are almost there.'

The boys, knowing that she could easily break down the tree if they refused, came down. They got into the basket, and soon she brought them to her home in the mountain. She set them down upon the ground and said,

'Now, boys, go and bring me a lot of wood, that I may make a fire in the oven and bake you some sweet cakes.'

The boys gathered a big pile of wood, with which she built a roaring fire in the adobe oven outside the house. Then she took them and washed them very carefully, and taking them by the necks, thrust them into the glowing oven and sealed the door with a great, flat rock, and left them there to be roasted.

But the Trues were friends of the Hero Twins, and did not let the heat harm them at all. When the old giant-woman had gone into the house, Maw-Sahv and Oo-yah-wee broke the smaller stone that closed the smoke-hole of the oven, and crawled out from their fiery prison unsinged. They ran around and caught snakes and toads and gathered up dirt and dropped them down into the oven through the smoke-hole; and then, watching when the giant-woman's back was turned, they sneaked into the house and hid in a huge clay jar on the shelf.

Very early in the morning the giant-woman's baby began to cry for some boy-meat.

'Wait till it is well cooked,' said the mother; and hushed the child till the sun was well up.

Then she went out and unsealed the oven, and brought in the sad mess the boys had put there.

'They have cooked away to almost nothing,' she said; and she and the giant-baby sat down to eat.

'Isn't this nice?' said the baby; and Maw-Sahv could not help saying,

'You nasty things, to like that!'

'Eh? Who is that?' cried the giant-woman, looking around till she found the boys hidden in the jar. So she told them to come down, and gave them some sweet cakes, and then sent them out to bring her some more wood.

It was evening when they returned with a big load of wood, which Maw-Sahv had taken pains to get green. He had also picked up in the mountains a long, sharp splinter of quartz. The evening was cool, and they built a big fire in the fireplace.

But immediately, as the boys had planned, the green wood began to smoke at a dreadful rate, and soon the room was so dense with it that they all began to cough and strangle. The giant-woman got up and opened the window and put her head out for a breath of fresh air; and Maw-Sahv, pulling out the white-hot splinter of quartz from the fire, stabbed her in the back so that she died. Then they killed the giant-baby, and at last felt that they were safe.

Now the giant-woman's house was a very large one, and ran far back into the very heart of the mountain. Having got rid of their enemies, the Hero Twins decided to explore the house; and, taking their bows and arrows, started boldly down into the deep, dark rooms. After travelling a long way in the dark, they came to a huge room in which corn and melons and pumpkins were growing abundantly.

On and on they went, till at last they heard the growl of distant thunder. Following the sound, they came presently to a room in the solid rock, wherein the lightning was stored. Going in, they took the lightning and played with it awhile, throwing it from one to the other, and at last started home, carrying their strange toy with them.

When they reached Acoma and told their grandmother of their wonderful adventures, she held up her withered old hands in amazement. And she was nearly scared to death when they began to play with the lightning, throwing it around the house as though it had been a harmless ball, while the thunder rumbled till it shook the great rock of Acoma. They had the blue lightning which belongs in the West; and the yellow lightning of the North; and the red lightning of the East; and the white lightning of the South; and with all these they played merrily.

But it was not very long till Shee-wo-nah, the Storm-king, had occasion to use the lightning; and when he looked in the room where he was wont to keep it, and found it gone, his wrath knew no bounds. He started out to find who had stolen it; and passing by Acoma he heard the thunder as the Hero Twins were playing ball with the lightning. He pounded on the door and ordered them to give him his lightning, but the boys refused. Then he summoned the storm, and it began to rain and blow fearfully outside; while within the boys rattled their thunder in loud defiance, regardless of their grandmother's entreaties to give the Storm-king his lightning.

It kept raining violently, however, and the water came pouring down the chimney until the room was nearly full, and they were in great danger of drowning. But luckily for them, the Trues were still mindful of them; and just in the nick of time sent their servant, Tee-oh-pee, the badger, who is the best of diggers, to dig a hole up through the floor; all the water ran out, and they were saved.

And so the Hero Twins outwitted the Storm-king.

South of Acoma, in the pine-clad gorges and mesas, the world was full of bears. There was one old She-Bear in particular, so huge and fierce that all men feared her; and not even the boldest hunter dared go to the south – for there she had her home with her two sons.

Maw-sahv and Oo-yah-wee were famous hunters, and always wished to go south; but their grandmother always forbade them.

One day, however, they stole away from the house, and got into the canon. At last they came to the she-bear's house; and there was old Quee-ah asleep in front of the door. Maw-sahv crept up very carefully and threw in her face a lot of ground chilli, and ran. At that the she-bear began to sneeze, ah-hutch! Ah-hutch! She could not stop, and kept making ah-hutch until she sneezed herself to death.

Then the Twins took their thunder-knives and skinned her. They stuffed the great hide with grass, so that it looked like a bear again, and tied a buckskin rope around its neck.

'Now,' said Maw-sahv, 'We will give our grandma a trick!'

So, taking hold of the rope, they ran toward Acoma, and the bear came behind them as if leaping. Their grandmother was going for water; and from the top of the cliff she saw them running so in the valley, and the bear jumping behind them. She ran to her house and painted one side of her face black with charcoal, and the other side red with the blood of an animal; and, taking a bag of ashes, ran down the cliff and out at the bear, to make it leave the boys and come after her.

But when she saw the trick, she reproved the boys for their rashness – but in her heart she was very proud of them.

From: Pueblo Indian Folk-Stories

The Disobedient Daughter Who Married a Skull

EFIONG EDEM WAS a native of Cobham Town. He had a very fine daughter, whose name was Afiong. All the young men in the country wanted to marry her on account of her beauty; but she refused all offers of marriage in spite of repeated entreaties from her parents, as she was very vain, and said she would only marry the best-looking man in the country, who would have to be young and strong, and capable of loving her properly.

Most of the men her parents wanted her to marry, although they were rich, were old men and ugly, so the girl continued to disobey her parents, at which they were very much grieved.

The skull who lived in the spirit land heard of the beauty of this Calabar virgin and thought he would like to possess her; so he went about amongst his friends and borrowed different parts of the body from them, all of the best. From one he got a good head, another lent him a body, a third gave him strong arms, and a fourth lent him a fine pair of legs. At last he was complete, and was a very perfect specimen of manhood. He then left the spirit land

and went to Cobham market, where he saw Afiong, and admired her very much.

About this time Afiong heard that a very fine man had been seen in the market, who was better looking than any of the natives. She therefore went to the market at once, and directly she saw the skull in his borrowed beauty, she fell in love with him, and invited him to her house. The skull was delighted, and went home with her, and on his arrival was introduced by the girl to her parents, and immediately asked their consent to marry their daughter. At first they refused, as they did not wish her to marry a stranger, but at last they agreed.

He lived with Afiong for two days in her parents' house, and then said he wished to take his wife back to his country, which was far off. To this the girl readily agreed, as he was such a fine man, but her parents tried to persuade her not to go.

However, being very headstrong, she made up her mind to go, and they started off together. After they had been gone a few days the father consulted his Ju Ju man, who by casting lots very soon discovered that his daughter's husband belonged to the spirit land, and that she would surely be killed.

They therefore all mourned her as dead.

After walking for several days, Afiong and the skull crossed the border between the spirit land and the human country. Directly they set foot in the spirit land, first of all one man came to the skull and demanded his legs, then another his head, and the next his body, and so on, until in a few minutes the skull was left by itself in all its natural ugliness. At this the girl was very frightened and wanted to return home, but the skull would not allow this, and ordered her to go with him.

When they arrived at the skull's house they found his mother, who was a very old woman quite incapable of doing any work, who could only creep about. Afiong tried her best to help her, and cooked her food, and brought water and firewood for the old woman. The old creature was very grateful for these attentions, and soon became quite fond of Afiong.

One day the old woman told Afiong that she was very sorry for her, but all the people in the spirit land were cannibals, and when they heard there was a human being in their country, they would come down and kill her and eat her. The skull's mother then hid Afiong, and as she had looked after her so well, she promised she would send her back to her country as soon as possible, providing that she promised for the future to obey her parents.

This Afiong readily consented to do.

Then the old woman sent for the spider, who was a very clever hairdresser, and made him dress Afiong's hair in the latest fashion. She also presented her with anklets and other things on account of her kindness. She then made a Ju Ju and called the winds to come and convey Afiong to her home. At first a violent tornado came, with thunder, lightning and rain, but the skull's mother sent him away as unsuitable. The next wind to come was a gentle breeze, so she told the breeze to carry Afiong to her mother's house, and said goodbye to her. Very soon afterwards, the breeze deposited Afiong outside her home, and left her there.

When the parents saw their daughter they were very glad, as they had for some months given her up as lost. The father spread soft animals' skins on the ground from where his daughter was standing all the way to the house, so that her feet should not be soiled. Afiong then walked to the house and her father called all the young girls who belonged to Afiong's company to come and dance, and the feasting and dancing was kept up for eight days and nights.

When the rejoicing was over, the father reported what had happened to the head chief of the town. The chief then passed a law that parents should never allow their daughters to marry strangers who came from a far country.

Then the father told his daughter to marry a friend of his, and she willingly consented, and lived with him for many years, and had many children.

From: Folk Stories from Southern Nigeria

The Enchanted Wine-jug

In ancient times there lived an old grey-haired man by the river's bank where the ferry boats land.

He was poor but honest, and being childless, and compelled to earn his own food, he kept a little wine-shop, which, small though it was, possessed quite a local reputation, for the aged proprietor would permit no quarrelling on his premises, and sold only one brand of wine, and this was of really excellent quality. He did not keep a pot of broth simmering over the coals at his door to tempt the passer-by, and thus increase his thirst on leaving

The old man rather preferred the customers who brought their little long-necked bottles, and carried the drink to their homes. There were some peculiarities – almost mysteries – about this little wine shop; the old man had apparently always been there, and had never seemed any younger. His wine never gave out, no matter how great might be the local thirst, yet he was never seen to make or take in a new supply; nor had he a great array of vessels in his shop.

On the contrary, he always seemed to pour the wine out of the one and same old bottle, the long, slender neck of which was black and shiny from being so often tipped in his old hand while the generous, warming stream gurgled outward to the bowl. This had long ceased to be a matter of inquiry, however, and only upon the advent of a stranger of an inquiring mind would the subject be re-discussed.

The neighbours were assured that the old man was thoroughly good, and that his wine was better. Furthermore, he sold it as reasonably as other men sold a much inferior article. And more than this, they did not care to know; or at least if they did once care, they had gotten over it, and were now content to let well enough alone.

I said the old man had no children. That is true, yet he had that which in a slight degree took the place of children, in that they were his daily care, his constant companions, and the partners of his bed and board. These deputy children were none other than a good-natured old dog, with laughing face and eyes, long silken ears that were ever on the alert, yet too soft to stand erect, a chunky neck, and a large round body covered with long soft tan hair and ending in a bushy tail.

He was the very impersonation of canine wisdom and good nature, and seldom became ruffled unless he saw his master worried by the ill behaviour of one of his patrons, or when a festive flea persisted in attacking him on all sides at once. His fellow, a cat, would sometimes assist in the onslaught, when the dog was about to be defeated and completely ruffled by his tormentor.

This 'Thomas' was also a character in his own way, and though past the days when his chief ambition had been to catch his tail, he had such a strong vein of humour running through him that age could not subdue his frivolous propensities. He had been known to drop a dead mouse upon the dog's nose from the counter, while the latter was endeavouring to get a quiet nap; and then he would blow his tail up as a balloon, hump his back, and look utterly shocked at such conduct, as the startled dog nearly jumped out of his skin, and growling horribly, tore around as though he were either in chase of a wild beast or being chased by one.

This happy couple lived in the greatest contentment with the old man. They slept in the little *kang* room with him at night, and enjoyed the warm stone floor, with its slick oil-paper covering, as much as did their master.

When the old man would go out on a mild moonlit night to enjoy a pipe of tobacco and gaze at the stars, his companions would rush out and announce to the world that they were not asleep, but ready to encounter any and every thing that the darkness might bring forth, so long as it did not enter their master's private court, of which they were in possession.

These two were fair-weather companions up to this time. They had not been with the old man when a bowl of rice was a luxury. Their days did not antedate the period of the successful wine shop history. The old man, however, often recalled those former days with a shudder, and thought with great complacency of the time when he had befriended a divine being, in the form of a weary human traveller, to whom he gave the last drink his jug contained, and how, when the contents of the little jug had gurgled down the stranger's throat in a long unbroken draught, the stranger had given him a trifling little thing that looked like a bit of amber, saying:

'Drop this into your jug, old man, and so long as it remains there, you will never want for a drink.'

He did so; and sure enough the jug was heavy with something, so that he raised it to his lips, and - could he believe it! a most delicious stream of wine poured down his parched throat.

He took the jug down and peered into its black depths; he shook its sides, causing the self within to dance and laugh aloud; and shutting his eyes, again he took another long draught; then meaning well, he remembered the stranger, and was about to offer him a drink, when he discovered that he was all alone, and began to wonder at the strange circumstance, and to think what he was to do.

'I can't sit here and drink all the time, or I will be drunk, and some thief will carry away my jug. I can't live on wine alone, yet I dare not leave this strange thing while I seek for work.'

Like many another to whom fortune has just come, he knew not for a time what to do with his good luck. Finally he hit upon the scheme of keeping a wine shop, the success of which we have seen, and have perhaps refused the old man credit for the wisdom he displayed in continuing on in a small scale, rather than in exciting unpleasant curiosity and official oppression, by turning up his jug and attempting to produce wine at wholesale. The dog and cat knew the secret, and had ever a watchful eye upon the jug, which was never for a moment out of sight of one of the three pairs of eyes.

As the brightest day must end in gloom, however, so was this pleasant state soon to be marred by a most sad and far-reaching accident.

One day the news flashed around the neighbourhood that the old man's supply of wine was exhausted; not a drop remained in his jug, and he had no more with which to refill it. Each man on hearing the news ran to see if it were indeed true, and the little straw-thatched hut and its small court encircled by a mud wall were soon filled with anxious seekers after the truth. The old man admitted the statement to be true, but had little to say; while the dog's ears hung neglected over his cheeks, his eyes dropped, and he looked as though he might be asleep, but for the persistent manner in which he refused to lie down, but dignifiedly bore his portion of the sorrow sitting upright, but with bowed head.

'Thomas' seemed to have been charged with agitation enough for the whole family. He walked nervously about the floor till he felt that justice to his tail demanded a higher plane, where shoes could not offend, and then betook himself to the counter, and later to the beam which supported the roof, and made a sort of cats' and rats' attic under the thatch.

All condoled with the old man, and not one but regretted that their supply of cheap, good wine was exhausted. The old man offered no explanation, though he had about concluded in his own mind that, as no one knew the secret, he must have in some way poured the bit of amber into a customer's jug. But who possessed the jug he could not surmise, nor could he think of any way of reclaiming it. He talked the matter over carefully and fully to himself at night, and the dog and cat listened attentively, winking knowingly at each other, and puzzling their brains much as to what was to be done and how they were to assist their kind old friend.

At last the old man fell asleep, and then sitting down face to face by his side, the dog and cat began a discussion.

'I am sure,' says the cat, 'that I can detect that thing if I only come within smelling distance of it; but how do we know where to look for it.'

That was a puzzler, but the dog proposed that they make a search through every house in the neighbourhood.

'We can go on a mere *kuh kyung* (look-see), you know, and while you call on the cats indoors, and keep your nostrils open, I will *yay gee* (chat) with the dogs outside, and if you smell anything you can tell me.'

The plan seemed to be the only good one, and it was adopted that very night. They were not cast down because the first search was unsuccessful, and continued their work night after night.

Sometimes their calls were not appreciated, and in a few cases they had to clear the field by battle before they could go on with the search. No house was neglected, however, and in due time they had done the whole neighbourhood, but with no success. They then determined that it must have been carried to the other side of the river, to which place they decided to extend their search as soon as the water was frozen over, so that they could cross on the ice, for they knew they would not be allowed in the crowded ferry-boats; and while the dog could swim, he knew that the water was too icy for that.

As it soon grew very cold, the river froze so solidly that bull-carts, ponies, and all passed over on the ice, and so it remained for near two months, allowing the searching party to return each morning to their poor old master, who seemed completely broken up by his loss, and did not venture away from his door, except to buy the few provisions which his little fund of savings would allow.

Time flew by without bringing success to the faithful comrades, and the old man began to think they too were deserting him, as his old customers had done. It was nearing the time for the spring thaw and freshet, when one night as the cat was chasing around over the roof timbers, in a house away to the outside of the settlement across the river, he detected an odour that caused him to stop so suddenly as to nearly precipitate himself upon a sleeping man on the floor below.

He carefully traced up the odour, and found that it came from a soapstone tobacco box that sat upon the top of a high clothes-press nearby.

The box was dusty with neglect, and 'Thomas' concluded that the possessor had accidentally turned the coveted gem (for it was from that the odour came) out into his wine bowl, and, not knowing its nature, had put it into this stone box rather than throw it away. The lid was so securely fastened that the box seemed to be one solid piece, and in despair of opening it, the cat went out to consult the superior wisdom of the dog, and see what could be done.

'I can't get up there,' said the dog, 'nor can you bring me the box, or I might break it.'

'I cannot move the thing, or I might push it off, and let it fall to the floor and break,' said the cat.

So after explaining the things they could not do, the dog finally hit upon a plan they might perhaps successfully carry out.

'I will tell you,' said he.

'You go and see the chief of the rat guild in this neighbourhood, tell him that if he will help you in this matter, we will both let him alone for ten years, and not hurt even a mouse of them.'

'But what good is that going to do?'

'Why, don't you see, that stone is no harder than some wood, and they can take turns at it till they gnaw a hole through, then we can easily get the gem.'

The cat bowed before the marvellous judgement of the dog, and went off to accomplish the somewhat difficult task of obtaining an interview with the master rat.

Meanwhile the dog wagged his ears and tail, and strode about with a swinging stride, in imitation of the great *yang ban*, or official, who occasionally walked past his master's door, and who seemed to denote by his haughty gait his superiority to other men. His importance made him impudent, and when the cat returned, to his dismay, he found his friend engaged in a genuine fight with a lot of curs who had dared to intrude upon his period of self-congratulation.

'Thomas' mounted the nearest wall, and howled so lustily that the inmates of the house, awakened by the uproar, came out and dispersed the contestants.

The cat had found the rat, who, upon being assured of safety, came to the mouth of his hole, and listened attentively to the proposition. It is needless to say he accepted it, and a contract was made forthwith. It was arranged that work was to begin at once, and be continued by relays as long as they could work undisturbed, and when the box was perforated, the cat was to be summoned.

The ice had now broken up and the pair could not return home very easily, so they waited about the neighbourhood for some months, picking up a scant living, and making many friends and not a few enemies, for they were a proud pair, and ready to fight on provocation.

It was warm weather, when, one night, the cat almost forgot his compact as he saw a big fat rat slinking along towards him. He crouched low and dug his long claws into the earth, while every nerve seemed on the jump; but before he was ready to spring upon his prey, he fortunately remembered his contract. It was just in time, too, for as the rat was none other than the other party to the contract, such a mistake at that time would have been fatal to their object.

The rat announced that the hole was completed, but was so small at the inside end that they were at a loss to know how to get the gem out, unless the cat could reach it with his paw. Having acquainted the dog with the good news, the cat hurried off to see for himself. He could introduce his paw, but as the object was at the other end of the box he could not quite reach it.

They were in a dilemma, and were about to give up, when the cat went again to consult with the dog. The latter promptly told them to put a mouse into the box, and let him bring out the gem. They did so, but the hole was too small for the little fellow and his load to get out at the same time, so that much pushing and pulling had to be done before they were successful. They got it safely at last, however, and gave it at once to the dog for safekeeping. Then, with much purring and wagging of tails, the contract of friendship was again renewed, and the strange party broke up; the rats to go and jubilant over their safety, the dog and cat to carry the good news to their mourning master.

Again canine wisdom was called into play in devising a means for crossing the river. The now happy dog was equal to such a trifling thing as this, however, and instructed the cat that he must take the gem in his mouth, hold it well between his teeth, and then mount the dog's back, where he could hold on firmly to the long hair of his neck while he swam across the river.

This was agreed upon, and arriving at the river they put the plan into execution. All went well until, as they neared the opposite bank, a party of school-children chanced to notice them coming, and, after their amazement at the strange sight wore away, they burst into uproarious laughter, which increased the more they looked at the absurd sight. They clapped their hands and danced with glee, while some fell on the ground and rolled about in an exhaustion of merriment at seeing a cat astride a dog's back being ferried across the river.

The dog was too weary, and consequently matter-of-fact, to see much fun in it, but the cat shook his sides till his agitation caused the dog to take in great gulps of water in attempting to keep his head up. This but increased the cat's merriment, till he broke out in a laugh as hearty as that of the children, and in doing so dropped the precious gem into the water. The dog, seeing the sad accident, dove at once for the gem; regardless of the cat, who could not let go in time to escape, and was dragged down under the water. Sticking his claws into the dog's skin, in his agony of suffocation, he caused him so much pain that he missed the object of his search, and came to the surface.

The cat got ashore in some way, greatly angered at the dog's rude conduct. The latter, however, cared little for that, and as soon as he had shaken the water from his hide, he made a lunge at his unlucky companion, who had lost the results of a half year's faithful work in one moment of foolishness.

Dripping like a drowned cat, 'Thomas' was, however, able to climb a tree, and there he stayed till the sun had dried the water from his fur, and he had spat the water from his inwards in the constant spitting he kept up at his now enemy, who kept barking ferociously about the tree below. The cat knew that the dog was dangerous when aroused, and was careful not to descend from his perch till the coast was clear; though at one time he really feared the ugly boys would knock him off with stones as they passed.

Once down, he has ever since been careful to avoid the dog, with whom he has never patched up the quarrel. Nor does he wish to do so, for the very sight of a dog causes him to recall that horrible cold ducking and the day spent up a tree, and involuntarily he spits as though still filled with river water, and his tail blows up as it had never learned to do till the day when for so long its damp and draggled condition would not permit of its assuming the haughty shape.

This accounts for the scarcity of cats and the popularity of dogs.

The dog did not give up his efforts even now. He dove many times in vain, and spent most of the following days sitting on the river's bank, apparently lost in thought. Thus the winter found him – his two chief aims apparently being to find the gem and to kill the cat. The latter kept well out of his way, and the ice now covered the place where the former lay hidden.

One day he espied a man spearing fish through a hole in the ice, as was very common. Having a natural desire to be around where anything eatable was being displayed, and feeling a sort of proprietorship in the particular part of the river where the man was fishing, and where he himself had had such a sad experience, he went down and looked on.

As a fish came up, something natural seemed to greet his nostrils, and then, as the man lay down his catch, the dog grabbed it and rushed off in the greatest haste. He ran with all his might to his master, who, poor man, was now at the end of his string (coins in Korea are perforated and strung on a string), and was almost reduced to begging. He was therefore delighted when his faithful old friend brought him so acceptable a present as a fresh fish. He at once commenced dressing it, but when he slit it open, to his infinite joy, his long-lost gem fell out of the fish's belly. The dog was too happy to contain himself, but jumping upon his master, he licked him with his tongue, and struck him with his paws, barking meanwhile as though he had again treed the cat.

As soon as their joy had become somewhat natural, the old man carefully placed the gem in his trunk, from which he took the last money he had, together with some fine clothes –relics of his more fortunate days. He had feared he must soon pawn these clothes, and had even shown them to the brokers.

But now he took them out to put them on, as his fortune had returned to him. Leaving the fish baking on the coals, he donned his fine clothes, and taking his last money, he went and purchased wine for his feast, and for a beginning; for he knew that once he placed the gem back in the jug, the supply of wine would not cease.

On his return he and the good dog made a happy feast of the generous fish, and the old man completely recovered his spirits when he had quaffed deeply of the familiar liquid to which his mouth was now such a stranger. Going to his trunk directly, he found to his amazement that it contained another suit of clothes exactly like the first ones he had removed, while there lay also a broken string of cash of just the amount which he had previously taken out.

Sitting down to think, the whole truth dawned upon him, and he then saw how he had abused his privilege before in being content to use his talisman simply to run a wine shop, while he might have had money and everything else in abundance by simply giving the charm a chance to work.

Acting upon this principle, the old man eventually became immensely wealthy, for he could always duplicate anything with his piece of amber. He carefully tended his faithful dog, who never in his remaining days molested a rat, and never lost an opportunity to attack every cat he saw.

From: Korean Tales

The Legend of the Wooden Shoe

IN YEARS LONG gone, too many for the almanac to tell of, or for clocks and watches to measure, millions of good fairies came down from the sun and went into the earth.

There, they changed themselves into roots and leaves, and became trees. There were many kinds of these, as they covered the earth, but the pine and birch, ash and oak, were the chief ones that made Holland. The fairies that lived in the trees bore the name of Moss Maidens, or Tree 'Trintjes,' which is the Dutch pet name for Kate, or Katharine.

The oak was the favourite tree, for people lived then on acorns, which they ate roasted, boiled or mashed, or made into meal, from which something like bread was kneaded and baked. With oak bark, men tanned hides and made leather, and, from its timber, boats and houses.

Under its branches, near the trunk, people laid their sick, hoping for help from the gods. Beneath the oak boughs, also, warriors took oaths to be faithful to their lords, women made promises, or wives joined hand in hand around its girth, hoping to have beautiful children. Up among its leafy branches the new babies lay, before they were found in the cradle by the other children. To make a young child grow up to be strong and healthy, mothers drew them through a split sapling or young tree. Even more wonderful, as medicine for the country itself, the oak had power to heal. The new land sometimes suffered from disease called the *val*. When sick with the *val*, the ground sunk. Then people, houses, churches, barns and cattle all went down, out of sight, and were lost forever, in a flood of water.

But the oak, with its mighty roots, held the soil firm. Stories of dead cities, that had tumbled beneath the waves, and of the famous Forest of Reeds, covering a hundred villages, which disappeared in one night, were known only too well.

Under the birch tree, lovers met to plight their vows, and on its smooth bark was often cut the figure of two hearts joined in one. In summer, the forest furnished shade, and in winter warmth from the fire. In the springtime, the new leaves were a wonder, and in autumn the pigs grew fat on the mast, or the acorns, that had dropped on the ground.

So, for thousands of years, when men made their home in the forest, and wanted nothing else, the trees were sacred.

But by and by, when cows came into the land and sheep and horses multiplied, more open ground was needed for pasture, grain fields and meadows. Fruit trees, bearing apples and pears, peaches and cherries, were planted, and grass, wheat, rye and barley were grown. Then, instead of the dark woods, men liked to have their gardens and orchards open to the sunlight. Still, the people were very rude, and all they had on their bare feet were rough bits of hard leather, tied on through their toes; though most of them went barefooted.

The forests had to be cut down. Men were so busy with the axe, that in a few years, the Wood Land was gone. Then the new 'Holland,' with its people and red roofed houses, with its chimneys and windmills, and dykes and storks, took the place of the old Holt Land of many trees.

Now there was a good man, a carpenter and very skilful with his tools, who so loved the oak that he gave himself, and his children after him, the name of Eyck, which is pronounced Ike, and is Dutch for oak. When, before his neighbours and friends, according to the beautiful Dutch custom, he called his youngest-born child, to lay the cornerstone of his new house, he bestowed upon her, before them all, the name of Neeltje Van Eyck.

The carpenter daddy continued to mourn over the loss of the forests. He even shed tears, fearing lest, by and by, there should not one oak tree be left in the country. Moreover, he was frightened at the thought that the new land, made by pushing back the ocean and building dykes, might sink down again and go back to the fishes. In such a case, all the people, the babies and their mothers, men, women, horses and cattle, would be drowned. The Dutch folks were a little too fast, he thought, in winning their acres from the sea.

One day, while sitting on his doorstep, brooding sorrowfully, a Moss Maiden and a Tree Elf appeared, skipping along, hand in hand. They came up to him and told him that his ancestral oak had a message for him. Then they laughed and ran away. Van Eyck, which was now the man's full family name, went into the forest and stood under the grand old oak tree, which his fathers loved, and which he would allow none to cut down.

Looking up, the leaves of the tree rustled, and one big branch seemed to sweep near him. Then it whispered in his ear:

'Do not mourn, for your descendants, even many generations hence, shall see greater things than you have witnessed. I and my fellow oak trees shall pass away, but the sunshine shall be spread over the land and make it dry. Then, instead of its falling down, like acorns from the trees, more and better food shall come up from out of the earth.

'Where green fields now spread, and the cities grow where forests were, we shall come to life again, but in another form. When most needed, we shall furnish you and your children and children's children, with warmth, comfort, fire, light, and wealth. Nor need you fear for the land, that it will fall; for, even while living, we, and all the oak trees that are left, and all the birch, beech, and pine trees shall stand on our heads for you. We shall hold up your houses, lest they fall into the ooze and you shall walk and run over our heads. As truly as when rooted in the soil, will we do this. Believe what we tell you, and be happy. We shall turn ourselves upside down for you.'

'I cannot see how all these things can be,' said Van Eyck.

'Fear not, my promise will endure.'

The leaves of the branch rustled for another moment. Then, all was still, until the Moss Maiden and Trintje, the Tree Elf, again, hand in hand, as they tripped along merrily, appeared to him.

'We shall help you and get our friends, the elves, to do the same. Now, do you take some oak wood and saw off two pieces, each a foot long. See that they are well-dried.

Then set them on the kitchen table tonight, when you go to bed.'

After saying this, and looking at each other and laughing, just as girls do, they disappeared.

Pondering on what all this might mean, Van Eyck went to his wood-shed and sawed off the oak timber. At night, after his wife had cleared off the supper table, he laid the foot-long pieces in their place.

When Van Eyck woke up in the morning, he recalled his dream, and, before he was dressed, hurried to the kitchen. There, on the table, lay a pair of neatly made wooden shoes. Not a sign of tools, or shavings could be seen, but the clean wood and pleasant odour made him glad.

When he glanced again at the wooden shoes, he found them perfectly smooth, both inside and out. They had heels at the bottom and were nicely pointed at the toes, and, altogether, were very inviting to the foot. He tried them on, and found that they fitted him exactly. He tried to walk on the kitchen floor, which his wife kept scrubbed and polished, and then sprinkled with clean white sand, with broomstick ripples scored in the layers, but for Van Eyck it was like walking on ice.

After slipping and balancing himself, as if on a tight rope, and nearly breaking his nose against the wall, he took off the wooden shoes, and kept them off, while inside the house. However, when he went outdoors, he found his new shoes very light, pleasant to the feet and easy to walk in. It was not so much like trying to skate, as it had been in the kitchen.

At night, in his dreams, he saw two elves come through the window into the kitchen. One, a kabouter, dark and ugly, had a box of tools. The other, a light-faced elf, seemed to be the guide. The kabouter at once got out his saw, hatchet, auger, long, chisel-like knife, and smoothing plane. At first, the two elves seemed to be quarrelling, as to who should be boss.

Then they settled down quietly to work.

The kabouter took the wood and shaped it on the outside. Then he hollowed out, from inside of it, a pair of shoes, which the elf smoothed and polished. Then one elf put his little feet in them and tried to dance, but he only slipped on the smooth floor and flattened his nose; but the other fellow pulled the nose straight again, so it was all right. They waltzed together upon the wooden shoes, then took them off, jumped out the window, and ran away.

When Van Eyck put the wooden shoes on, he found that out in the fields, in the mud, and on the soft soil, and in sloppy places, this sort of foot gear was just the thing. They did not sink in the mud and the man's feet were comfortable, even after hours of labour. They did not 'draw' his feet, and they kept out the water far better than leather possibly could.

When the Van Eyck *vrouw* and the children saw how happy Daddy was, they each one wanted a pair. Then they asked him what he called them.

'Klompen,' said he, in good Dutch, and klompen, or klomps, they are to this day.

'I'll make a fortune out of this,' said Van Eyck.

'I'll set up a klomp-winkel, a shop for wooden shoes at once.'

So, going out to the blacksmith's shop, in the village, he had the man who pounded iron fashion for him on his anvil, a set of tools, exactly like those used by the kabouter and the elf, which he had seen in his dream.

Then he hung out a sign, marked 'Wooden blocks for shoes.' He made klomps for the little folks just out of the nursery, for boys and girls, for grown men and women, and for all who walked out-of-doors, in the street or on the fields.

Soon klomps came to be the fashion in all the country places. It was good manners, when you went into a house, to take off your wooden shoes and leave them at the door. Even in the towns and cities, ladies wore wooden slippers, especially when walking or working in the garden.

Klomps also set the fashion for soft, warm socks, and stockings made from sheep's wool. Soon, a thousand needles were clicking, to put a soft cushion between one's soles and toes and the wood. Women knitted, even while they walked to market, or gossiped on the streets. The klomp-winkels, or shops of the shoe carpenters, were seen in every village.

When rich beyond his daydreams, Van Eyck had another joyful night vision. The next day, he wore a smiling countenance. Everybody, who met him on the street, saluted him and asked, in a neighbourly way:

'Good morning, Mynheer Bly-moe-dig, Mr. Cheerful. How do you sail today?'

That's the way the Dutch talk: not 'how do you do,' but, in their watery country, it is this,

'How do you sail?' or else,

'Hoe gat het u al?' (How goes it with you, already?)

Then Van Eyck told his dream. It was this: The Moss Maiden and Trintje, the wood elf, came to him again at night and danced. They were lively and happy.

'What now?' asked the dreamer, smilingly, of his two visitors.

He had hardly got the question out of his mouth, when in walked a kabouter, all smutty with blacksmith work. In one hand, he grasped his toolbox. In the other, he held a curious-looking machine. It was a big lump of iron, set in a frame, with ropes to pull it up and let it fall down with a thump.

'What is it?' asked Van Eyck.

'It's a Hey,' (a pile driver), said the kabouter, showing him how to use it.

'When men say to you, on the street, tomorrow, "How do you sail?" laugh at them,' said the Moss Maiden, herself laughing.

'Yes, and now you can tell the people how to build cities, with mighty churches with lofty towers, and with high houses like those in other lands. Take the trees, trim the branches off, sharpen the tops, turn them upside down and pound them deep in the ground. Did not the ancient oak promise that the trees would be turned upside down for you? Did they not say you could walk on top of them?'

By this time, Van Eyck had asked so many questions, and kept the elves so long, that the Moss Maiden peeped anxiously through the window. Seeing the day breaking, she and Trintje and the kabouter flew away, so as not to be petrified by the sunrise.

'I'll make another fortune out of this, also,' said the happy man, who, next morning, was saluted as Mynheer Blydschap, Mr. Joyful.

At once, Van Eyck set up a factory for making pile drivers. Sending men into the woods, who chose the tall, straight trees, he had their branches cut off.

Then he sharpened the trunks at one end, and these were driven, by the pile driver, down, far and deep, into the ground. So a foundation, as good as stone, was made in the soft and spongy soil, and well-built houses by the thousands. Even the lofty walls of churches stood firm. The spires were unshaken in the storm.

Old Holland had not fertile soil like France, or vast flocks of sheep, producing wool, like England, or armies of weavers, as in the Belgic lands. Yet, soon there rose large cities, with splendid mansions and town halls. As high towards heaven as the cathedrals and towers in other lands, which had rock for foundation, her brick churches rose in the air.

On top of the forest trees, driven deep into the sand and clay, dams and dykes were built, that kept out the ocean. So, instead of the old two thousand square miles, there were, in the realm, in the course of years, twelve thousand, rich in green fields and cattle.

Then, for all the boys and girls that travel in this land of quaint customs, Holland was a delight.

From: Dutch Fairy Tales for Young Folks

Rabbit & the Moon-man

Once, long ago, Rabbit lived with his old grandmother deep in the Canadian forest, far from all other people. He was a great hunter, and all around, far and near, he laid snares and set traps to catch game for food.

It was winter, and he caught many little animals and birds. He brought them home daily to feed himself and his old grandmother, and he was well pleased with his success. But after some weeks had passed he was unable to catch any game.

He always found his traps and snares empty, although many tracks were always around them, and there were many signs that animals were prowling about. He knew then that he was being robbed nightly, and that a thief was pilfering his traps. It was very cold and the snow lay deep in the forest, and Rabbit and his old grandmother were in dire need of food.

Every morning Rabbit rose very early and hurried off to his traps, but always he found them empty, for the thief had been ahead of him. He was greatly puzzled, for he could not think who the thief was.

At last one morning, after a new fall of snow, he found the mark of a long foot near his traps, and he knew it was the foot of the game-robber. It was the longest footprint he had ever seen, long and narrow and very light, like a moonbeam.

And Rabbit said,

'Now I shall rise earlier in the morning, and I shall go to my traps ahead of the thief and take my game, so that they will all be empty when he comes.'

Each morning he rose earlier to catch the thief, but the man of the long foot was always there before him, and his game was always gone. No matter how early Rabbit got up, the thief was always ahead of him and his traps were always empty.

So Rabbit said to his old grandmother,

'The man of the long foot, who robs my traps, is always up ahead of me, no matter how early I rise. I will make a snare from a bow-string, and I will watch all this night, and I will surely catch him.'

He made a trap from a stout bow-string and set it beside his snares, and took the end of the bow-string some distance away to a clump of trees, behind which he hid. He hoped that the thief would step into the trap; then he would pull the bow-string and tie him fast to a tree. He sat very quiet, waiting for the man of the long foot to appear. It was moonlight when he set out, but soon it grew very dark in the forest.

The Moon suddenly disappeared. But the stars were all shining on the white snow and there were no clouds in the sky, and Rabbit wondered what had happened to the Moon. He waited very still and a little frightened in the starlight.

Soon he heard someone coming, sneaking stealthily through the trees. Then he saw a white light which dazzled his eyes. The light went towards the snares, until it stopped just at the trap Rabbit had set.

Then Rabbit pulled the bow-string, closed the trap as he had hoped, and tied the string fast to a tree. He heard sounds of a struggle, and he saw the white light move from side to side, but he knew that he had his prisoner fast and that the man of the long foot was caught at last.

He was much afraid of the white light, and he ran home as fast as he could and told his old grandmother that he had caught the game-robber in the trap, and that he did not know who he was, for he was too frightened to look.

And his grandmother said,

'You must go back and see who it is, and tell him he must stop robbing your snares.'

But Rabbit said,

'I do not want to go until daylight, for the Moon has gone down and the forest is very dark.'

But his grandmother said,

'You must go.'

So poor Rabbit, although he was very frightened by what he had seen, set out again for his traps.

When he drew near to his snares he saw that the white light was still shining. It was so bright that his eyes were dazzled and he had to stop far from it. Then he approached nearer, but his eyes soon became very sore. There was a stream flowing beside him, and he bathed his eyes in the cold water, but it brought him no relief, and his eyes felt hot and red, and tears fell from them because of the dazzling light.

Then he took great handfuls of snow and threw snowballs at the light, hoping thereby to put it out. But when the snowballs came near to the light they melted and fell down like rain. Then, with his eyes still smarting, Rabbit in his rage scooped up great handfuls of soft black mud from the bottom of the stream, and forming it into balls, he threw them with all his force at the white light.

He heard them strike something with a dull thud, and he heard loud yells from the prisoner – the man of the long foot – behind the shining light.

Then a voice came from the light, saying,

'Why did you snare me? Come and untie me at once. I am the Man in the Moon. It is near to the morning, and before dawn I must be on my way home. You have already spotted my face with mud, and if you do not loose me at once I shall kill all your tribe.'

Poor Rabbit was more frightened than before, and he ran home and told his old grandmother what had happened. And his grandmother was also very frightened, for she thought that no good could come of it. And she told Rabbit to go back at once and untie the Man in the Moon, for the night was almost spent, and the dawn would soon be breaking.

So poor Rabbit, trembling in his fear, went back to his traps. From a great distance he cried,

'I will untie you if you will never again rob my snares, and if you will never come back to earth.'

And the prisoner in the trap promised, and said,

'I swear it by my white light.'

Then Rabbit approached very carefully. He had to shut his eyes and grope his way because of the bright light, and his lip quivered because of the great heat. At last he rushed in and cut the bow-string snare with his teeth, and the Man in the Moon hurried on his way, for he could already see the dawn in the East.

But Rabbit was almost blinded while he was about it, and his shoulders were badly scorched. And ever since that time Rabbit blinks and his eyelids are pink, and water runs from his eyes when he looks at a bright light; and his lip always quivers; and his shoulders are yellow, even when he wears his white winter coat, because of the great light and heat on the winter night long ago when he loosened the Man in the Moon from the snare.

And since that night the Man in the Moon has never come back to earth. He stays at his task in the sky, lighting the forest by night; but he still bears on his face the marks of the black mud which Rabbit threw at him. And sometimes for several nights he goes away to a quiet place, where he tries to wash off the mud; and then the land is dark. But he never succeeds in cleaning himself, and when he comes back to his work the marks of Rabbit's mud-balls are still upon his shining face.

From: Canadian Fairy Tales

The Story of Ivan & the Daughter of the Sun

THERE WERE ONCE upon a time four brethren, and three of them remained at home, while the fourth went out to seek for work.

This youngest brother came to a strange land, and hired himself out to a husbandman for three gold pieces a year. For three years he served his master faithfully, so, at the end of his time, he departed with nine gold pieces in his pocket.

The first thing he now did was to go to a spring, and into this spring he threw three of his gold pieces.

'Let us see now,' said he, 'if I have been honest, they will come swimming back to me.'

Then he lay down by the side of the spring and went fast asleep.

How long he slept there, who can tell? but at any rate he woke up at last and went to the spring, but there was no sign of his money to be seen.

Then he threw three more of the gold pieces into the spring, and again he lay down by the side of it and slept.

Then he got up and went and looked into the spring, and still there was no sign of the money.

So he threw in his three remaining gold pieces, and again lay down and slept.

The third time he arose and looked into the spring, and there, sure enough, was his money: all nine of the gold pieces were floating on the surface of the water!

And now his heart felt lighter, and he gathered up the nine gold pieces and went on his way. On the road he fell in with three *katsapi* with a laden wagon. He asked them concerning their wares, and they said they were carrying a load of incense. He begged them straightway to sell him this incense.

Then they sold it to him for the gold pieces, and when he had bought it and they had departed, he kindled fire and burnt the incense, and offered it up to God as a sweet-smelling sacrifice.

Then an angel flew down to him, and said,

'Oh, thou that hast offered this sweet-smelling sacrifice to God, what dost thou want for thine own self? Dost thou want a tsardom, or great riches? Or, perchance, the desire of thy heart is a good wife? Speak, for God will give thee whatsoever thou desirest.'

When the man had listened to the angel, he said to him,

'Tarry a while! I will go and ask those people who are ploughing yonder.'

Now those people who were ploughing there were his own brethren, but he did not know that they were his brethren. So he went up and said to the elder brother,

Tell me, uncle, what shall I ask of God? A tsardom, or great riches, or a good wife? Tell me, which of the three is the best gift to ask for?'

And his eldest brother said to him,

'I know not, and who does know? Go and ask someone else.'

So he went to the second brother, who was ploughing a little farther on. He asked him the same question, but the man only shrugged his shoulders and said he didn't know either. Then he went to the third brother, who was the youngest of the three, and also ploughing there.

And he asked him, saying,

'Tell me, now, which is the best gift to ask of God: a tsardom, or great riches, or a good wife?'

And the third brother said,

'What a question! Thou art too young for a tsardom, and great riches last but for a little while; ask God for a good wife, for if it please God to give thee a good wife, 'tis a gift that will bless thee all thy life long.'

So he went back to the angel and asked for a good wife. Then he went on his way till he came to a certain wood, and, looking about him, he perceived that in this wood was a lake. And while he was looking at it, three wild doves came flying along and lit down upon this lake.

They threw off their plumage and plunged into the water, and then he saw that they were not wild doves, but three fair ladies. They bathed in the lake, and in the meantime the youth crept up and took the raiment of one of them and hid it behind the bushes.

When they came out of the water the third lady missed her clothes. Then the youth said to her,

'I know where thy clothes are, but I will not give them to thee unless thou wilt be my wife.'

'Good!' cried she, 'thy wife will I be.'

Then she dressed herself, and they went together to the nearest village.

When they got there, she said to him,

'Now go to the nobleman who owns the land here, and beg him for a place where we may build us a hut.'

So he went right up to the nobleman's castle and entered his reception room, and said, 'Glory be to God!'

'Forever and ever!' replied the nobleman.

'What dost thou want here, Ivan?'

'I have come, sir, to beg of thee a place where I may build me a hut.'

'A place for a hut, eh? Good, very good. Go home, and I'll speak to my overseer, and he shall appoint thee a place.'

So he returned from the nobleman's castle, and his wife said to him,

'Go now into the forest and cut down an oak, a young oak, that thou canst span round with both arms.'

So he cut down such an oak as his wife had told him of, and she built a hut of the oak, for the overseer had come and shown them a place where they might build their hut. But when the overseer returned home he praised loudly to his master the wife of this Ivan.

'She is such and such,' said he.

'Fair she may be,' replied the nobleman, 'but she is another's.'

'She need not be another's for long,' replied the overseer. 'This Ivan is in our hands; let us send him to see why it is the sun grows so red when he sets.'

'That's just the same as if you sent him to a place whence he can never return.'

'All the better.'

Then they sent for Ivan, and gave him this errand, and he returned home to his wife, weeping bitterly.

Then his wife asked him all about it, and said,

'Well, I can tell thee all about the ways of the sun, for I am the sun's own daughter. So now I'll tell thee the whole matter. Go back to this nobleman and say to him that the reason why the sun turns so red as he sets is this: Just as the sun is going down into the sea, three fair ladies rise out of it, and it is the sight of them which makes him turn so red all over!'

So he went back and told them.

'Oh-ho!' cried they, 'if you can go as far as that, you may now go a little farther'; so they told him to go to hell and see how it was there.

'Yes,' said his wife, 'I know the road that leads to hell also very well; but the nobleman must let his overseer go with thee, or else he never will believe that thou really didst go to hell.'

So the nobleman told his overseer that he must go to hell too, so they went together; and when they got there the rulers of hell laid hands upon the overseer straightway.

'Thou dog!' roared they, 'we've been looking out for thee for some time!'

So Ivan returned without the overseer, and the nobleman said to him,

'Where's my overseer?'

'I left him in hell,' said Ivan, 'and they said there that they were waiting for you, sir, too.'

When the nobleman heard this he hanged himself, but Ivan lived happily with his wife.

From: Cossack Fairy Tales & Folk Tales

The Ivory City & Its Fairy Princess

One day a young prince was out practising archery with the son of his father's chief vizier, when one of the arrows accidentally struck the wife of a merchant, who was walking about in an upper room of a house close by.

The prince aimed at a bird that was perched on the windowsill of that room, and had not the slightest idea that anybody was at hand, or he would not have shot in that direction. Consequently, not knowing what had happened, he and the vizier's son walked away, the vizier's son chaffing him because he had missed the bird.

Presently the merchant went to ask his wife about something, and found her lying, to all appearance, dead in the middle of the room, and an arrow fixed in the ground within half a yard of her head. Supposing that she was dead, he rushed to the window and shrieked,

'Thieves, thieves! They have killed my wife.'

The neighbours quickly gathered, and the servants came running upstairs to see what was the matter. It happened that the woman had fainted, and that there was only a very slight wound in her breast where the arrow had grazed.

As soon as the woman recovered her senses she told them that two young men had passed by the place with their bows and arrows, and that one of them had most deliberately aimed at her as she stood by the window.

On hearing this the merchant went to the king, and told him what had taken place. His majesty was much enraged at such audacious wickedness, and swore that most terrible punishment should be visited on the offender if he could be discovered. He ordered the merchant to go back and ascertain whether his wife could recognise the young men if she saw them again.

'Oh yes,' replied the woman, 'I should know them again among all the people in the city.'

'Then,' said the king, when the merchant brought back this reply, 'tomorrow I will cause all the male inhabitants of this city to pass before your house, and your wife will stand at the window and watch for the man who did this wanton deed.'

A royal proclamation was issued to this effect. So the next day all the men and boys of the city, from the age of ten years upwards, assembled and marched by the house of the merchant. By chance (for they both had been excused from obeying this order) the king's son and the vizier's son were also in the company, and passed by in the crowd. They came to see the tamasha.

As soon as these two appeared in front of the merchant's window they were recognised by the merchant's wife, and at once reported to the king.

'My own son and the son of my chief vizier!' exclaimed the king, who had been present from the commencement. 'What examples for the people! Let them both be executed.'

'Not so, your majesty,' said the vizier, 'I beseech you let the facts of the case be thoroughly investigated. How is it?' he continued, turning to the two young men. 'Why have you done this cruel thing?'

'I shot an arrow at a bird that was sitting on the sill of an open window in yonder house, and missed,' answered the prince. 'I suppose the arrow struck the merchant's wife. Had I known that she or anybody had been near I should not have shot in that direction.'

'We will speak of this later on,' said the king, on hearing this answer. 'Dismiss the people. Their presence is no longer needed.'

In the evening his majesty and the vizier had a long and earnest talk about their two sons. The king wished both of them to be executed; but the vizier suggested that the prince should be banished from the country.

This was finally agreed to.

Accordingly, on the following morning, a little company of soldiers escorted the prince out of the city.

When they reached the last custom-house the vizier's son overtook them. He had come with all haste, bringing with him four bags of muhrs on four horses.

'I am come,' he said, throwing his arms round the prince's neck, 'because I cannot let you go alone. We have lived together, we will be exiled together, and we will die together.

Turn me not back, if you love me.'

'Consider,' the prince answered, 'what you are doing. All kinds of trial may be before me. Why should you leave your home and country to be with me?'

'Because I love you,' he said, 'and shall never be happy without you.'

So the two friends walked along hand in hand as fast as they could to get out of the country, and behind them marched the soldiers and the horses with their valuable burdens. On reaching a place on the borders of the king's dominions the prince gave the soldiers some gold, and ordered them to return. The soldiers took the money and left; they did not, however, go very far, but hid themselves behind rocks and stones, and waited till they were quite sure that the prince did not intend to come back.

On and on the exiles walked, till they arrived at a certain village, where they determined to spend the night under one of the big trees of the place. The prince made preparations for a fire, and arranged the few articles of bedding that they had with them, while the vizier's son went to the baniya and the baker and the butcher to get something for their dinner.

For some reason he was delayed; perhaps the tsut was not quite ready, or the baniya had not got all the spices prepared. After waiting half an hour the prince became impatient, and rose up and walked about.

He saw a pretty, clear little brook running along not far from their resting place, and hearing that its source was not far distant, he started off to find it. The source was a beautiful lake, which at that time was covered with the magnificent lotus flower and other water plants. The prince sat down on the bank, and being thirsty took up some of the water in his hand.

Fortunately he looked into his hand before drinking, and there, to his great astonishment, he saw reflected whole and clear the image of a beautiful fairy. He looked around, hoping to see the reality; but seeing no person, he drank the water, and put out his hand to take some more. Again he saw the reflection in the water which was in his palm. He looked around as before, and this time discovered a fairy sitting by the bank on the opposite side of the lake. On seeing her he fell so madly in love with her that he dropped down in a swoon.

When the vizier's son returned, and found the fire lighted, the horses securely fastened, and the bags of muhrs lying altogether in a heap, but no prince, he did not know what to think. He waited a little while, and then shouted; but not getting any reply, he got up and went to the brook. There he came across the footmarks of his friend. Seeing these, he went back at once for the money and the horses, and bringing them with him, he tracked the prince to the lake, where he found him lying to all appearance dead.

'Alas! Alas!' he cried, and lifting up the prince, he poured some water over his head and face.

'Alas! My brother, what is this? Oh! Do not die and leave me thus. Speak, speak! I cannot bear this!'

In a few minutes the prince, revived by the water, opened his eyes, and looked about wildly.

'Thank God!' exclaimed the vizier's son. 'But what is the matter, brother?'

'Go away,' replied the prince. 'I don't want to say anything to you, or to see you. Go away.'

'Come, come; let us leave this place. Look, I have brought some food for you, and horses, and everything. Let us eat and depart.'

'Go alone,' replied the prince.

'Never,' said the vizier's son. 'What has happened to suddenly estrange you from me? A little while ago we were brethren, but now you detest the sight of me.'

'I have looked upon a fairy,' the prince said. 'But a moment I saw her face; for when she noticed that I was looking at her she covered her face with lotus petals. Oh, how beautiful she was! And while I gazed she took out of her bosom an ivory box, and held it up to me. Then I fainted. Oh! If you can get me that fairy for my wife, I will go anywhere with you.'

'Oh, brother,' said the vizier's son, 'you have indeed seen a fairy. She is a fairy of the fairies. This is none other than Gulizar of the Ivory City. I know this from the signs that she gave you. From her covering her face with lotus petals I learn her name, and from her showing you the ivory box I learn where she lives. Be patient, and rest assured that I will arrange your marriage with her.'

When the prince heard these encouraging words he felt much comforted, rose up, and ate, and then went away gladly with his friend.

On the way they met two men.

These two men belonged to a family of robbers. There were eleven of them altogether. One, an elder sister, stayed at home and cooked the food, and the other ten – all brothers – went out, two and two, and walked about the four different ways that ran through that part of the country, robbing those travellers who could not resist them, and inviting others, who were too powerful for two of them to manage, to come and rest at their house, where the whole family attacked them and stole their goods.

These thieves lived in a kind of tower, which had several strong-rooms in it, and under it was a great pit, wherein they threw the corpses of the poor unfortunates who chanced to fall into their power.

The two men came forward, and, politely accosting them, begged them to come and stay at their house for the night.

'It is late,' they said, 'and there is not another village within several miles.'

'Shall we accept this good man's invitation, brother?' asked the prince.

The vizier's son frowned slightly in token of disapproval; but the prince was tired, and thinking that it was only a whim of his friend's, he said to the men,

'Very well. It is very kind of you to ask us.'

So they all four went to the robbers' tower.

Seated in a room, with the door fastened on the outside, the two travellers bemoaned their fate.

'It is no good groaning,' said the vizier's son.

'I will climb to the window, and see whether there are any means of escape. Yes! yes!' he whispered, when he had reached the window-hole.

'Below there is a ditch surrounded by a high wall. I will jump down and reconnoitre. You stay here, and wait till I return.'

Presently he came back and told the prince that he had seen a most ugly woman, whom he supposed was the robbers' housekeeper. She had agreed to release them on the promise of her marriage with the prince.

So the woman led the way out of the enclosure by a secret door.

'But where are the horses and the goods?' the vizier's son inquired.

'You cannot bring them,' the woman said.

'To go out by any other way would be to thrust oneself into the grave.'

'All right, then; they also shall go out by this door. I have a charm, whereby I can make them thin or fat.'

So the vizier's son fetched the horses without any person knowing it, and repeating the charm, he made them pass through the narrow doorway like pieces of cloth, and when they were all outside restored them to their former condition. He at once mounted his horse and laid hold of the halter of one of the other horses, and then beckoning to the prince to do likewise, he rode off. The prince saw his opportunity, and in a moment was riding after him, having the woman behind him.

Now the robbers heard the galloping of the horses, and ran out and shot their arrows at the prince and his companions. And one of the arrows killed the woman, so they had to leave her behind.

On, on they rode, until they reached a village where they stayed the night. The following morning they were off again, and asked for Ivory City from every passerby. At length they came to this famous city, and put up at a little hut that belonged to an old woman, from whom they feared no harm, and with whom, therefore, they could abide in peace and comfort. At first the old woman did not like the idea of these travellers staying in her house, but the sight of a muhr, which the prince dropped in the bottom of a cup in which she had given him water, and a present of another muhr from the vizier's son, quickly made her change her mind. She agreed to let them stay there for a few days.

As soon as her work was over the old woman came and sat down with her lodgers. The vizier's son pretended to be utterly ignorant of the place and people.

'Has this city a name?' he asked the old woman.

'Of course it has, you stupid. Every little village, much more a city, and such a city as this, has a name.'

'What is the name of this city?'

'Ivory City. Don't you know that? I thought the name was known all over the world.'

On the mention of the name Ivory City the prince gave a deep sigh. The vizier's son looked as much as to say,

'Keep quiet, or you'll discover the secret.'

'Is there a king of this country?' continued the vizier's son.

'Of course there is, and a queen, and a princess.'

'What are their names?'

'The name of the princess is Gulizar, and the name of the queen.'

The vizier's son interrupted the old woman by turning to look at the prince, who was staring like a madman.

'Yes,' he said to him afterwards, 'we are in the right country. We shall see the beautiful princess.'

One morning the two travellers noticed the old woman's most careful toilette: how careful she was in the arrangement of her hair and the set of her kasabah and puts.

'Who is coming?' said the vizier's son.

'Nobody,' the old woman replied.

'Then where are you going?'

'I am going to see my daughter, who is a servant of the Princess Gulizar. I see her and the princess every day. I should have gone yesterday, if you had not been here and taken up all my time.'

'Ah-h-h! Be careful not to say anything about us in the hearing of the princess.'

The vizier's son asked her not to speak about them at the palace, hoping that, because she had been told not to do so, she would mention their arrival, and thus the princess would be informed of their coming.

On seeing her mother the girl pretended to be very angry.

'Why have you not been for two days?' she asked.

'Because, my dear,' the old woman answered, 'two young travellers, a prince and the son of some great vizier, have taken up their abode in my hut, and demand so much of my attention. It is nothing but cooking and cleaning, and cleaning and cooking, all day long. I can't understand the men,' she added; 'one of them especially appears very stupid. He asked me the name of this country and the name of the king. Now where can these men have come from, that they do not know these things? However, they are very great and very rich. They each give me a muhr every morning and every evening.'

After this the old woman went and repeated almost the same words to the princess, on the hearing of which the princess beat her severely; and threatened her with a severer punishment if she ever again spoke of the strangers before her.

In the evening, when the old woman had returned to her hut, she told the vizier's son how sorry she was that she could not help breaking her promise, and how the princess had struck her because she mentioned their coming and all about them.

'Alas! Alas!' said the prince, who had eagerly listened to every word. 'What, then, will be her anger at the sight of a man?'

'Anger?' said the vizier's son, with an astonished air. 'She would be exceedingly glad to see one man. I know this. In this treatment of the old woman I see her request that you will go and see her during the coming dark fortnight.'

'Heaven be praised!' the prince exclaimed.

The next time the old woman went to the palace Gulizar called one of her servants and ordered her to rush into the room while she was conversing with the old woman; and if the old woman asked what was the matter, she was to say that the king's elephants had gone mad, and were rushing about the city and bazaar in every direction, and destroying everything in their way.

The servant obeyed, and the old woman, fearing lest the elephants should go and push down her hut and kill the prince and his friend, begged the princess to let her depart. Now Gulizar had obtained a charmed swing, that landed whoever sat on it at the place wherever they wished to be.

'Get the swing,' she said to one of the servants standing by.

When it was brought she bade the old woman step into it and desire to be at home.

The old woman did so, and was at once carried through the air quickly and safely to her hut, where she found her two lodgers safe and sound.

'Oh!' she cried, 'I thought that both of you would be killed by this time. The royal elephants have got loose and are running about wildly. When I heard this I was anxious about you. So the princess gave me this charmed swing to return in. But come, let us get outside before the elephants arrive and batter down the place.'

'Don't believe this,' said the vizier's son. 'It is a mere hoax. They have been playing tricks with you.'

'You will soon have your heart's desire,' he whispered aside to the prince. 'These things are signs.'

Two days of the dark fortnight had elapsed, when the prince and the vizier's son seated themselves in the swing, and wished themselves within the grounds of the palace. In a moment they were there, and there too was the object of their search standing by one of the palace gates, and longing to see the prince quite as much as he was longing to see her.

Oh, what a happy meeting it was!

'At last,' said Gulizar, 'I have seen my beloved, my husband.'

'A thousand thanks to Heaven for bringing me to you,' said the prince.

Then the prince and Gulizar betrothed themselves to one another and parted, the one for the hut and the other for the palace, both of them feeling happier than they had ever been before.

Henceforth the prince visited Gulizar every day and returned to the hut every night. One morning Gulizar begged him to stay with her always. She was constantly afraid of some evil happening to him – perhaps robbers would slay him, or sickness attack him, and then she would be deprived of him.

She could not live without seeing him. The prince showed her that there was no real cause for fear, and said that he felt he ought to return to his friend at night, because he had left his home and country and risked his life for him; and, moreover, if it had not been for his friend's help he would never have met with her.

Gulizar for the time assented, but she determined in her heart to get rid of the vizier's son as soon as possible. A few days after this conversation she ordered one of her maids to make a pilaw. She gave special directions that a certain poison was to be mixed into it while cooking, and as soon as it was ready the cover was to be placed on the saucepan, so that the poisonous steam might not escape. When the pilaw was ready she sent it at once by the hand of a servant to the vizier's son with this message:

'Gulizar, the princess, sends you an offering in the name of her dead uncle.'

On receiving the present the vizier's son thought that the prince had spoken gratefully of him to the princess, and therefore she had thus remembered him. Accordingly he sent back his salam and expressions of thankfulness.

When it was dinnertime he took the saucepan of pilaw and went out to eat it by the stream. Taking off the lid, he threw it aside on the grass and then washed his hands. During the minute or so that he was performing these ablutions, the green grass under the cover of the saucepan turned quite yellow. He was astonished, and suspecting that there was poison in the pilaw, he took a little and threw it to some crows that were hopping about. The moment the crows ate what was thrown to them they fell down dead.

'Heaven be praised,' exclaimed the vizier's son, 'who has preserved me from death at this time!'

On the return of the prince that evening the vizier's son was very reticent and depressed. The prince noticed this change in him, and asked what was the reason.

'Is it because I am away so much at the palace?'

The vizier's son saw that the prince had nothing to do with the sending of the pilaw, and therefore told him everything.

'Look here,' he said, 'in this handkerchief is some pilaw that the princess sent me this morning in the name of her deceased uncle. It is saturated with poison. Thank Heaven, I discovered it in time!'

'Oh, brother! who could have done this thing? Who is there that entertains enmity against you?'

'The Princess Gulizar. Listen. The next time you go to see her, I entreat you to take some snow with you; and just before seeing the princess put a little of it into both your eyes. It will provoke tears, and Gulizar will ask you why you are crying. Tell her that you weep for the loss of your friend, who died suddenly this morning. Look! Take, too, this wine and this shovel, and when you have feigned intense grief at the death of your friend, bid the princess to drink a little of the wine. It is strong, and will immediately send her into a deep sleep. Then, while she is asleep, heat the shovel and mark her back with it.

Remember to bring back the shovel again, and also to take her pearl necklace. This done, return. Now fear not to execute these instructions, because on the fulfilment of them depends your fortune and happiness. I will arrange that your marriage with the princess shall be accepted by the king, her father, and all the court.'

The prince promised that he would do everything as the vizier's son had advised him; and he kept his promise.

The following night, on the return of the prince from his visit to Gulizar, he and the vizier's son, taking the horses and bags of muhrs, went to a graveyard about a mile or so distant. It was arranged that the vizier's son should act the part of a fakir and the prince the part of the fakir's disciple and servant.

In the morning, when Gulizar had returned to her senses, she felt a smarting pain in her back, and noticed that her pearl necklace was gone. She went at once and informed the king of the loss of her necklace, but said nothing to him about the pain in her back.

The king was very angry when he heard of the theft, and caused proclamation concerning it to be made throughout all the city and surrounding country.

'It is well,' said the vizier's son, when he heard of this proclamation. 'Fear not, my brother, but go and take this necklace, and try to sell it in the bazaar.'

The prince took it to a goldsmith and asked him to buy it.

'How much do you want for it?' asked the man.

'Fifty thousand rupees,' the prince replied.

'All right,' said the man; 'wait here while I go and fetch the money.'

The prince waited and waited, till at last the goldsmith returned, and with him the kotwal, who at once took the prince into custody on the charge of stealing the princess's necklace.

'How did you get the necklace?' the kotwal asked.

'A fakir, whose servant I am, gave it to me to sell in the bazaar,' the prince replied. 'Permit me, and I will show you where he is.'

The prince directed the kotwal and the policeman to the place where he had left the vizier's son, and there they found the fakir with his eyes shut and engaged in prayer. Presently, when he had finished his devotions, the kotwal asked him to explain how he had obtained possession of the princess's necklace.

'Call the king hither,' he replied, 'and then I will tell his majesty face to face.'

On this some men went to the king and told him what the fakir had said. His majesty came, and seeing the fakir so solemn and earnest in his devotions, he was afraid to rouse his anger, lest peradventure the displeasure of Heaven should descend on him, and so he placed his hands together in the attitude of a supplicant, and asked,

'How did you get my daughter's necklace?'

'Last night,' replied the fakir, 'we were sitting here by this tomb worshipping Khuda, when a ghoul, dressed as a princess, came and exhumed a body that had been buried a few days ago, and began to eat it. On seeing this I was filled with anger, and beat her back with a shovel, which lay on the fire at the time. While running away from me her necklace got loose and dropped. You wonder at these words, but they are not difficult to prove. Examine your daughter, and you will find the marks of the burn on her back. Go, and if it is as I say, send the princess to me, and I will punish her.'

The king went back to the palace, and at once ordered the princess's back to be examined.

'It is so,' said the maidservant; 'the burn is there.'

'Then let the girl be slain immediately,' the king shouted.

'No, no, your majesty,' they replied.

'Let us send her to the fakir who discovered this thing, that he may do whatever he wishes with her.'

The king agreed, and so the princess was taken to the graveyard.

'Let her be shut up in a cage, and be kept near the grave whence she took out the corpse,' said the fakir.

This was done, and in a little while the fakir and his disciple and the princess were left alone in the graveyard. Night had not long cast its dark mantle over the scene when the fakir and his disciple threw off their disguise, and taking their horses and luggage, appeared before the cage.

They released the princess, rubbed some ointment over the scars on her back, and then sat her upon one of their horses behind the prince. Away they rode fast and far, and by the morning were able to rest and talk over their plans in safety. The vizier's son showed the princess some of the poisoned pilaw that she had sent him, and asked whether she had repented of her ingratitude.

The princess wept, and acknowledged that he was her greatest helper and friend.

A letter was sent to the chief vizier telling him of all that had happened to the prince and the vizier's son since they had left their country.

When the vizier read the letter he went and informed the king. The king caused a reply to be sent to the two exiles, in which he ordered them not to return, but to send a letter to Gulizar's father, and inform him of everything. Accordingly they did this; the prince wrote the letter at the vizier's son's dictation.

On reading the letter Gulizar's father was much enraged with his viziers and other officials for not discovering the presence in his country of these illustrious visitors, as he was especially anxious to ingratiate himself in the favour of the prince and the vizier's son. He ordered the execution of some of the viziers on a certain date.

'Come,' he wrote back to the vizier's son, 'and stay at the palace. And if the prince desires it, I will arrange for his marriage with Gulizar as soon as possible.'

The prince and the vizier's son most gladly accepted the invitation, and received a right noble welcome from the king. The marriage soon took place, and then after a few weeks the king gave them presents of horses and elephants, and jewels and rich cloths, and bade them start for their own land; for he was sure that the king would now receive them.

The night before they left the viziers and others, whom the king intended to have executed as soon as his visitors had left, came and besought the vizier's son to plead for them, and promised that they each would give him a daughter in marriage. He agreed to do so, and succeeded in obtaining their pardon.

Then the prince, with his beautiful bride Gulizar, and the vizier's son, attended by a troop of soldiers, and a large number of camels and horses bearing very much treasure, left for their own land. In the midst of the way they passed the tower of the robbers, and with the help of the soldiers they razed it to the ground, slew all its inmates, and seized the treasure which they had been amassing there for several years.

At length they reached their own country, and when the king saw his son's beautiful wife and his magnificent retinue he was at once reconciled, and ordered him to enter the city and take up his abode there.

Henceforth all was sunshine on the path of the prince. He became a great favourite, and in due time succeeded to the throne, and ruled the country for many, many years in peace and happiness.

From: Indian Fairy Tales

The Death 'Bree'

THERE WAS ONCE a woman, who lived in the Camp-del-more of Strathavon, whose cattle were seized with a murrain, or some such fell disease, which ravaged the neighbourhood at the time, carrying off great numbers of them daily.

All the forlorn fires and hallowed waters failed of their customary effects; and she was at length told by the wise people, whom she consulted on the occasion, that it was evidently the effect of some infernal agency, the power of which could not be destroyed by any other means than the never-failing specific – the juice of a dead head from the churchyard, – a nostrum certainly very difficult to be procured, considering that the head must needs be abstracted from the grave at the hour of midnight.

Being, however, a woman of a stout heart and strong faith, native feelings of delicacy towards the sanctuary of the dead had more weight than had fear in restraining her for some time from resorting to this desperate remedy. At length, seeing that her stock would soon be annihilated by the destructive career of the disease, the wife of Camp-del-more resolved to put the experiment in practice, whatever the result might be.

Accordingly, having with considerable difficulty engaged a neighbouring woman as her companion in this hazardous expedition, they set out a little before midnight for the parish churchyard, distant about a mile and a half from her residence, to execute her determination. On arriving at the churchyard her companion, whose courage was not so notable, appalled by the gloomy prospect before her, refused to enter among the habitations of the dead. She, however, agreed to remain at the gate till her friend's business was accomplished.

This circumstance, however, did not stagger the wife's resolution. She, with the greatest coolness and intrepidity, proceeded towards what she supposed an old grave, took down her spade, and commenced her operations. After a good deal of toil she arrived at the object of her labour.

Raising the first head, or rather skull, that came in her way, she was about to make it her own property, when a hollow, wild, sepulchral voice exclaimed,

'That is my head; let it alone!' Not wishing to dispute the claimant's title to this head, and supposing she could be otherwise provided, she very good-naturedly returned it and took up another.

'That is my father's head,' bellowed the same voice.

Wishing, if possible, to avoid disputes, the wife of Campdel-more took up another head, when the same voice instantly started a claim to it as his grandfather's head.

'Well,' replied the wife, nettled at her disappointments, 'although it were your grandmother's head, you shan't get it till I am done with it.'

'What do you say, you limmer?' says the ghost, starting up in his awry habiliments.

'What do you say, you limmer?' repeated he in a great rage. 'By the great oath, you had better leave my grandfather's head.'

Upon matters coming this length, the wily wife of Camp-del-more thought it proper to assume a more conciliatory aspect. Telling the claimant the whole particulars of the predicament in which she was placed, she promised faithfully that if his honour would only allow her to carry off his grandfather's skull or head in a peaceable manner, she would restore it again when done with.

Here, after some communing, they came to an understanding; and she was allowed to take the head along with her, on condition that she should restore it before cock-crowing, under the heaviest penalties.

On coming out of the churchyard and looking for her companion, she had the mortification to find her 'without a mouthful of breath in her body'; for, on hearing the dispute between her friend and the guardian of the grave, and suspecting much that she was likely to share the unpleasant punishments with which he threatened her friend, at the bare recital of them she fell down in a faint, from which it was no easy matter to recover her.

This proved no small inconvenience to Camp-del-more's wife, as there were not above two hours to elapse ere she had to return the head according to the terms of her agreement.

Taking her friend upon her back, she carried her up a steep acclivity to the nearest adjoining house, where she left her for the night; then repaired home with the utmost speed, made *dead bree* of the head ere the appointed time had expired, restored the skull to its guardian, and placed the grave in its former condition. It is needless to add that, as a reward for her exemplary courage, the '*bree*' had its desired effect.

The cattle speedily recovered, and, so long as she retained any of it, all sorts of diseases were of short duration.

From: Folk-lore & Legends: Scotland

Finis

Workbooks From The Scheherazade Foundation

We hope that you have enjoyed this collection of stories, gleaned from varying cultural corners of the world, and that you have been entertained by them.

But, have you considered the deeper meanings and interwoven layers that lie hidden beneath the surface?

At The Scheherazade Foundation, we believe that Teaching-Stories contain wisdom, information, and marvels that have the power to transform the way we think, and thereby change our lives.

Employed as a bedrock of culture throughout the centuries – challenging established patterns of thinking, while passing on knowledge and values – tales such as the ones contained in this volume are a rich resource ready and waiting to be mined.

As an aid to help in the perception of less-obvious facets and layers, we have created a series of original Workbooks. Aimed at stimulating thought-provoking discussions and igniting deep reflection, these tools will assist in unlocking the power of Teaching-Stories.

www.ingramcontent.com/pod-product-compliance
Lightning Source LLC
Chambersburg PA
CBHW020321030826
48979CB00022B/663

* 9 7 8 1 9 1 5 3 1 1 4 0 5 *